C030

A Sharp Rise in Crime

Other Roger West books

A Sharp Rise In Crime

by

John Creasey

The 43rd book of Roger West of the Yard

CHARLES SCRIBNER'S SONS

NEW YORK

Copyright © 1978 The Estate of John Creasey

Library of Congress Cataloging in Publication Data

Creasey, John.
    A sharp rise in crime.

    I. Title.
PZ3.C86153Shf 1978   [PR6005.R517]   823'.9'12   78-11132
ISBN 0-684-14921-4

1 3 5 7 9 11 13 15 17 19 O/C 20 18 16 14 12 10 8 6 4 2

Printed in the United States of America

Contents

A Sharp Rise in Crime

1

The Man Who Looked Like West

'IT'S UNCANNY,' SAID Partridge, of South West Division.

'Never seen anything like it,' remarked Calk, of North East.

'You mean you've seen *two* like it,' cackled Spettlebury of Central, and he gave a roar of laughter.

The five men present all joined in; it wasn't such a good joke but these men, Divisional leaders in the Criminal Investigation Department of the Metropolitan Police in London, were all tense; keyed-up. They were discussing a series of crimes and their own failure to solve them, and they were under pressure from their superior officers at the Yard to get results.

Partridge, big and bony, with a slippery Adam's apple, was the first to stop laughing.

He did not just laugh less heartily; he stopped, abruptly enough for all the others to stare at him; and soon the last murmurs of laughter in the old-fashioned office in Clapham died away.

The office was in a large Victorian house, taken over recently by the police because the local police stations were bursting at the seams. From four tall windows the trees of Clapham Common could be seen. They, the grass and the shrubs and the hedges were all the pale green of spring; the husks which had confined the seeds dropping and blowing in the soft wind.

This was mid-morning in early May; most children were at school and only the very young were out there, skipping, running and laughing; or the elderly, moving slowly, while others were to be seen sitting on the freshly-painted benches enjoying the late spring sunshine.

Spettlebury, large and over-fat, a two-chinned, heavy-paunched man, was the first to ask: 'What's on your mind, Birdy?'

Superintendent James Partridge said: 'Forget it.'

'We want to know.' That was Calk, an average-looking man with no special characteristics unless it were the brightness of eyes against a deeply tanned skin. Calk spent every minute he could on the golf course or tennis court.

'Let's have it,' urged the fourth man present.

He was Superintendent Trannion – they were all superintendents, meeting in secret conclave to discuss this particular problem. One of his greatest assets as a policeman was that he looked like an old Testament patriarch, with his long, silvery hair and his low-pitched melodious voice. In some ways he not only looked, but played, the part. Trannion had never been heard to swear; he did not smoke; he would have a drink on special occasions but was not really a drinker. If he womanised it was one of the Yard's best kept secrets, and the Yard was not remarkable for the ease with which members could keep such information from others.

Those who did not actively like him, respected him.

'You really ought to tell us why you suddenly stopped laughing,' he urged.

'Seized with a great idea.' That was O'Malley, the Cockney Irishman, as likely as anyone to bring a quick laugh; he was a man of medium height whose face was so deeply lined one wondered how he could ever shave into those deep crevices. 'This man's the spitting image of our Handsome West. *I* think that's a joke. What stopped making it funny to you, Birdy?'

Partridge still hesitated, and it was Trannion who broke the silence. At his first word all of the others turned towards him. A bird flew against the window, but did not seem hurt; every eye turned towards the window and then back to Trannion, who had broken off as if glad of a chance to marshal his words more carefully.

'Jim, are you implying that it is conceivable that there are not two men, but one?'

'My Gawd!' breathed O'Malley.

None of the others spoke; not even Partridge.

'Perhaps I should put it more plainly still,' went on Trannion. 'Are you implying that Handsome West might be leading a double life?'

'It's bloody nonsense,' rasped O'Malley.

'Be quiet, Pat, please.' Trannion's rebuke was as gentle as his voice but his face was set and his expression stern. 'Jim, you owe us a reply, you know. Everything said in this room is confidential, and —'

'Crap!' exclaimed O'Malley.

'And exactly what do you mean by that?' demanded Trannion, patiently.

'I mean that if we thought there was a chance in a thousand of West being this other guy we'd have to tell Coppell, pretty damned quick. That's how confidential it is. And lemme tell you another thing —'

'I'm not sure we need a monologue from you.'

Trannion's voice had an edge to it, as if he knew he had been caught in error and resented it.

'Well, you're going to hear what I think about it, Matt, whether you like it or not.' The 'Matt' was obviously intended as an olive branch, O'Malley did not want the five men to break up in bad-tempered disagreement. 'I think if Birdy or you or anyone else has got any evidence that West is a two-timing crook in his spare time, we ought to hear it, and if we agree on its importance, we ought to report it to Coppell or the A.C. *Today*. But if it's just some bloody silly idea that's crossed Birdy's mind, then let's forget it. I don't believe West would touch anything crooked with a barge-pole, but that doesn't mean there isn't some evidence that ought to be sifted. *And* I'd be the first to sift it. *That's* what I want to say.' O'Malley settled back in his chair, then took a small cigarette-making machine and a plastic pouch from his pocket, and began to roll a cigarette out of tobacco which looked like curly clips of black hair. It was in fact dark shag.

'That's how I feel,' remarked Calk.

'I don't see how anyone could quarrel with the reasoning,' Trannion said, grasping O'Malley's olive branch with both hands. 'What do you think, Spettlebury?'

It was a strange fact that only a few intimates called Spettlebury 'Jack'; his surname was used by nearly all of his fellow superintendents, and it was a measure of the fact that despite his fatness, his outward geniality and his ready mirth he was not on intimate terms with anybody at the Yard. Once, years earlier, there had been a move to call him the 'Loner' but Spettlebury he remained.

'I would want some convincing evidence,' he replied.

'So we are all in agreement on that score,' declared Trannion, who had become an unofficial chairman. '*Have* you any evidence, Birdy? Or was it just a flash thought?'

Birdy Partridge still did not reply but his Adam's apple was moving up and down at startling speed. It emphasised a thin and scraggy neck, while implying that his remark about West was much more than just a flash thought.

Suddenly, he said:'I need to think about this more.'

'Then think aloud,' urged O'Malley.

'I am not sure that would be wise,' said Trannion, in his most conciliatory manner. 'After all, we have to remember that we are discussing a senior officer in the Force, the associate of us all and friend of most, probably the best-known policeman in the country and the man who has, whether we like it or not, done more to improve the image of the police with the general public than anyone else.'

He paused as if to give the others a chance to disagree, but none did; in fact, O'Malley muttered, 'I'll say,' and Spettlebury said: 'There's no doubt about that.'

'So let us carry the present situation a stage further,' went on Trannion, earnestly. 'We all of us know that much of the crime in London has been organised extremely well lately and we believe that a single individual, operating a Mafia-like organisation with an extensive knowledge of London and its environs, is mainly responsible. He works of course through night clubs and turf accountants, and it is increasingly apparent that he extorts what is called 'protection' money from these establishments, as well as from the legalised gambling clubs and casinos.' He paused again, before asking: 'Is that a fair summing up?'

'Fair enough,' Calk said.

'When are you going to start telling us something we don't know?' demanded O'Malley.

'Patience, Pat, patience. We have attempted the normal method of dealing with this situation and failed utterly.' Trannion's voice held the relish of a religious orator pronouncing doom. He went on: 'We placed three of our more promising officers, two men and one young woman, in gambling clubs where each might have a chance to learn and perhaps even see this unknown man, and—'Trannion placed the tips of his fingers together, and closed his eyes before adding in a whisper, ' – all – three – have – been – murdered.'

There was a moment of silence, then Trannion's eyes, shut for a moment as if in silent prayer, shot open. They were steel-grey and they flashed in the light, while his voice gathered force until it rang through the room.

'They must be avenged. And we are the avengers!'

Again, there was silence – before O'Malley put in, as matter-of-fact as only a Cockney could be: 'Cool it, Matt – we're cops. We catch the killers, the judge takes the vengeance.' It was like a douse of cold water and did a great deal to break the tension which Trannion had managed to create. 'We don't know for sure that these three got close to the chap—'

'We do know they were all murdered!'

'And they each had their throat cut,' stated Spettlebury.

'Ear to ear,' Calk said easily, making the situation even more macabre than it was already.

'And we also know that Detective Officer Alice Brace posted this photograph to us before she died, and wrote on the back: "99 per cent virtually certain this is the invisible man".

The picture was of a man in bed, naked from the waist up, smiling – as if in invitation to whoever was taking the picture. None of these five police officers could be sure, but there seemed a real possibility that Alice Brace was going beyond – as they might say in the services – beyond the call of duty to get the evidence that this man was Mr Invisible. For his arms were held out, and he was smiling: a very handsome man indeed.

*   *   *

She had been going 'beyond the call of duty'.

She was an attractive young woman in the middle-twenties, and she had known lovers; and she knew that this man was a very great lover.

She wondered, as she moved slowly, tantalisingly, towards him, whether he would tire of her before she found out all she needed – as a policewoman – to know.

She also wondered what would happen if he knew that actually inside her bra there was a tiny camera, which took pictures as she unfastened the hooks and eyes at the back.

Next day, she had the negatives developed; but only the one she had sent to Trannion had been of any use.

Before he had received it, her body had been found floating in the Thames near Chelsea Bridge; but she had died of a slashed carotid artery, not of drowning.

*   *   *

The photograph had been enlarged and a hundred copies of it had been made; one was in front of each of the five men round the table at the house in Clapham. The talking had stopped, and now Birdy Partridge was gulping more than ever, as if his thoughts were passing very swiftly through his mind but were still not clear enough to formulate.

'Perhaps we should adjourn for a meal,' Trannion suggested. 'It's getting pretty late—'

Partridge stated with great deliberation: 'It *could* be West.'

'We all know that,' said Spettlebury.

'I don't,' O'Malley said, harshly.

'It could be West because of that scar under his chin,' said Partridge; his voice squeaked, his Adam's apple raced.

'Scar?' cried Calk. 'Where?'

'Look under the chin on the left-hand side of the picture,' urged Partridge. 'It's a faint, triangular scar. See it?'

O'Malley muttered: 'It's a flaw in the print.'

'I see it!' exclaimed Calk.

'There is undoubtedly some kind of a mark,' Trannion agreed.

'Can't really miss it once your attention's been drawn to it,' declared Spettlebury. 'And has Handsome West got a scar there?'

'*I've* never seen one,' said O'Malley.

'Nor I,' said Calk.

'But I have – I was there when he was chasing some men over a junk yard in the East End and fell on a piece of metal. It was damned lucky for him it didn't puncture his neck. Anyway he had to have two or three stitches in it, and there are dozens of men at the Yard who know it happened. It was seeing that scar which shook me up just now.'

'In these circumstances—' Trannion began.

'Two people could have a scar in the same place,' growled O'Malley.

'Indubitably,' agreed Trannion, 'but this is sufficient *prima facie* evidence to present to the Commander. Surely no one can disagree with that.' He looked around at all four, his gaze lingering longest on O'Malley, who scowled uneasily.

'Then it only remains to be decided who presents the report and whether it should be by word of mouth, or in writing signed by us all,' went on Trannion, and again he looked from one to the other, obviously expecting to be nominated to convey the report, and as obviously astounded when Spettlebury said:

'There's one thing we could do first, Matt, and I'd like to do it.'

And what is that?' asked Trannion, sternly.

'Have a talk with West himself and ask what he has to say about it,' said Spettlebury, flatly.

2

Majority Report

AS SPETTLEBURY'S VOICE faded there was absolute silence; almost, it might be said, a stunned silence. Another bird flew against the window but this time none of the men took any notice. Into the silence came the harsh ringing of the telephone bell, and Trannion gave a *tcha-tcha* of annoyance.

'Superintendent Trannion,' he announced, and after a second of listening he straightened up in his chair. 'Yes, sir. . . Yes, we have been discussing the one matter since nine o'clock. . . I don't think we can say we have reached any positive conclusion as to the best method of approach, but. . . I *do* realise that the matter is urgent. We all do.' He raised his eyes as if invoking sympathy from heaven. 'I think we may have a set of proposals by the middle of the afternoon.'

He stopped; frowning. There was a faint echo of a voice from the other end of the telephone. Trannion's brows drew together until there was a deep groove between his eyes, and his lips set in a thin line before he said in a very cold voice: 'That is quite impossible, sir. . . I am sorry, but it is not practicable to set a deadline on such an issue. . . I think it possible that by the middle of the afternoon our deliberations will have led us to some positive proposals, but pressure from the

Commissioner and from the Home Secretary himself certainly will not help us to reach objective decisions – on the contrary such pressure could easily lead to the wrong actions through over-hasty conclusions.'

He stopped; and now all the men in the room could hear the voice at the other end of the line, and knew that it was Commander Coppell of the Criminal Investigation Department, and a man before whom most officers, even seniors, often quaked.

The shouting ceased.

'Commander,' said Superintendent Trannion icily, 'if we have a report for you by four o'clock this afternoon it will be because the circumstances make it possible, *not* because the Home Secretary is displeased. Goodbye, sir.'

He rang off.

He must have been aware of the way all the others were staring at him, but he seemed more preoccupied with what had just been said, and his expression and the corrugations on his brow were positively thunderous.

'Matthew,' O'Malley said, 'I take my hat off to you.'

'Eh? Oh. Thank you. But really, the Commander should know better than to try to panic me into making decisions. Do they really think we must jump to a governmental command? That would make us a police state – very little better anyhow.' Trannion placed a clenched fist on the table, but his expression gradually softened, and when he spoke again it was in a much calmer voice. 'Now gentlemen – we need to allow our subconscious minds to work. Can we get lunch sent up here, Birdy, or should we go across to your canteen?'

'Neither,' Birdy Partridge answered. 'There's a

private hotel round the corner and they're fixing lunch for us. Can't have a private room, but the dining-room is big enough to talk without the danger of being overheard.'

'Do us good to talk about something else,' declared Trannion. 'I trust the food will be passable.'

'The landlady makes the best steak pudding in London,' boasted Birdy.

'Then you should have more of it,' retorted Trannion. 'You might get a little more flesh on your bones!'

There was a general laugh.

'They've a licence for beer and wines, no hard liquor,' Partridge said with a look of apology at the others.

'Wine at noon maketh the mind dull,' declared Trannion, 'and I don't drink anyhow, so it couldn't be better.' He managed to put them into a good frame of mind, which stayed throughout a lunch of steak and kidney pudding, followed by lemon meringue pie and a cheese board which would have done credit to any restaurant in London. They lingered only for a few minutes over coffee, and were back at the oval table by two o'clock.

Immediately, the mood changed, even though Trannion asked drily: "Well, how have our sub-consciouses been working?"

Partridge said: 'We can't possibly tell West.'

'Why the devil not?' demanded O'Malley.

'Because if he's guilty he'll be warned.'

'Or cover himself completely,' observed Trannion. 'Surely all these things go without saying. If West – if any man in such circumstances – were given the slightest warning that he was suspected, then we would lose all advantage of surprise.'

'You could tell in a moment if he were lying,' O'Malley said.

'No, Pat,' reasoned Trannion. 'If he is such a practised deceiver as to be both running with the hare and with the hounds, then he certainly won't give himself away when asked a direct question. You are fooling yourself if you think he would.'

'*I* happen to think he's an honest man,' O'Malley declared defiantly.

'Of all the men at the Yard, not excluding ourselves, I think I trust West more than anyone but—' Trannion shrugged as he looked apologetically at O'Malley. 'I think the others are right, Pat. It seemed a good idea, but I don't think it is, really. So we have a vote of four-to-one that we should point out this scar to the Commander and tell him that we think West should be investigated.'

Calk and Spettlebury nodded and Partridge said clearly: 'Yes.'

Trannion looked at O'Malley appealingly, and put all the pleading he could into his voice.

'Won't you make it unanimous, Pat?'

'No. I won't.'

'After all, it's only a recommendation.'

'I put in a minority report,' interrupted O'Malley, the stubborn look on his face matching the gravity of Trannion's, 'that we talk to West before this accusation is made. And that's final.' He leaned back in his chair and thrust his hands deep in his pockets.

'Then the four to one recommendation stands,' said Trannion. He looked about him with a rather elaborate display of assumed surprise. 'You would like *me* to present it, wouldn't you? – but my goodness, we haven't yet decided whether it's to be written or oral.'

'Oral,' Spettlebury said.

'Agreed,' said Calk.

'Only way,' asserted Partridge.

'Tell you one thing.' O'Malley perked up; he was never in low spirits for long, and now his eyes had a merry gleam. 'If we make it a written report each of us will have to read and approve and sign. It could take a heck of a long time to prepare. I once knew a man, he was one of the best conmen I ever put inside, who could argue for an hour about where to put a comma. How about writing the report, Matt, and we could hold it over until the morning. Easy.'

'Pat,' Calk reproved, 'this isn't a joke.'

'You're telling me that it's not a joke to accuse Handsome of—'

'No one is accusing Handsome of anything,' interrupted Trannion, in his most reasoning voice. 'And you know that the Commander wouldn't stand for that. There's no reason why we shouldn't wait until four o'clock, though, and keep him waiting for a while.'

'No.' Spettlebury was surprisingly sharp. 'We've decided what to do. Let's do it. I move Matthew to be our spokesman.'

'Remember it's a minority report.' O'Malley was resentful again.

'I will tell the Commander exactly what you think as well as speak for the others. Thank you for the confidence you have reposed in me.' Trannion pushed his chair back and stood up, looking more like an Old Testament prophet than ever. 'Would you like to meet again after I've seen the Commander?'

'Just let us know,' Partridge said, and almost under his breath he muttered: 'I wish to God I hadn't noticed that scar.'

No one else spoke.

Trannion, whose divisional headquarters was only a mile away, telephoned for a car, and was the last but one to leave. When at last his car arrived, he asked Partridge: 'Will you tell Coppell to expect me in about half-an-hour?'

'Yes,' Partridge promised, through a scowl; and then he asked in a troubled voice: 'You don't think there can possibly be any truth in this, do you?'

'Whatever we think personally, we have to make sure,' Trannion said in his most pontifical way. 'Where is West, do you know?'

Partridge muttered: 'Yes.'

'Where?'

'Having a day off with wife. Gone to a matinée, I think, and then going out to dinner.' He rubbed his bony chin, while Trannion watched as if commanding him to go on: 'Goes around town a lot more with her than he used to.'

'Indeed,' said Trannion, as if the announcement had great significance.

'Yes, he – well, one of his sons emigrated to Australia, and the other's making a name for himself in television – researching, I think they call it, and directing. What I mean is, Handsome doesn't have the expenses he used to have, and his wife was always at him to take her out more. I mean – he *can* afford it, in the circumstances, even out of his salary.'

'If that question arises I shall put the point of view to the Commander,' Trannion promised, solemnly; and then he turned and got into his car.

*   *   *

At that very moment Roger was sitting back in the. Dress Circle of the Adelphi Theatre, roaring with laughter. Janet, his wife, was laughing too, though not quite so hilariously. The matinée audience seemed about equally divided between those who were laughing their heads off, and those who found nothing remotely funny in the antics on the stage. This was a revival of a Tom Walls and Ralph Lynn farce.

Now and again Janet glanced at her husband.

He was taking life much more easily than she could remember, and the Yard was not working him anything like as hard as it had once done. As far as she was concerned, he could stay in the Police Force for ever if there were no pressures worse than the present ones; that is, if he could take her to the theatre occasionally and they could dine out without being interrupted by an emergency call from the Yard.

One of the actors, wearing a shirt and socks, made a sudden dive under the bed; the door opened and his wife came in, leading another man by the hand. Those who found this funny simply raised the roof, those who found it flat and dull stared glumly.

'And remember, dearest,' the wife said earnestly, 'if you hear the slightest noise, just dive under the bed.'

'Sweetheart,' Roger West said a few moments later, 'I don't know why I find it so funny, but I do. I – oh, *lorrrrd!*' He doubled up again.

It was five o'clock when they left the theatre, Roger a tall, powerful man who was startlingly good-looking; better looking, many women said, now that he had matured, than when he had been younger. Hardly a woman in the foyer or in the street outside failed to look at him. Janet, knowing this well, knowing that in the trendy talk of the day her Roger could be called a sex symbol, was fully aware and completely untroubled. She was a head shorter than he was, as dark as he was fair, with the sparkling eyes and slim figure a woman fifteen years younger might well have envied.

'Shall we go and get some tea somewhere near?' Roger asked.

'Darling, I feel extravagant,' Janet said. 'Let's get a taxi and go to the Dorchester. They still serve the nicest tea in London.'

'Then the Dorchester it shall be,' Roger decided, and raised a hand for a passing cab.

*   *   *

A uniformed policeman saw, recognised and heard him.

A plain-clothes detective sergeant, there about a hotel theft nearby, saw, recognised and heard him.

Both men used almost the same phrase to themselves.

'Handsome's living it up, these days.'

*   *   *

Chief Detective Superintendent Trannion and Commander Coppell made a striking contrast. Trannion, austere, ascetic; Coppell, big, heavy-shouldered, nearly ugly, with a pock-marked and swarthy complexion where Trannion's was fresh and wholesome-looking. Coppell was now sitting behind a big square-topped desk in a room in New Scotland Yard, while Trannion sat at ease opposite him. There was in both men a mood of 'I'm as good as the next', and this showed in their expressions, as Coppell listened, stirring occasionally in his swivel chair, obviously exerting all his self-control not to interrupt. And he succeeded, not saying a word until Trannion stated: 'Four of us thought we should come straight to you, sir. One was of the opinion that we ought to see West first.'

'Who was that?' demanded Coppell in a deep, rough voice.

'Is that relevant, sir?'

'Like hell it's relevant. Anyone who would warn West mustn't be allowed to get within a hundred yards of him. Was it O'Malley?'

'Yes,' Trannion answered reluctantly.

'Did anyone else show any particular sympathy for West? And I *mean* sympathy.'

'No,' answered Trannion with great deliberation. 'Everyone was shocked and found it hard to believe the evidence could really mean what it appeared to mean but there was no—' He hesitated before going on: 'I don't think 'sympathy' is the word which applies here, sir. I think four of us admitted feeling suspicion, no matter how reluctantly, and O'Malley refused to. But even he said that it had to be checked out.'

'Nice of him,' growled Coppell. 'Talked to anyone else?'

'About *this,* sir?'

'What the hell do you think I mean?'

Trannion sat back in his chair and did not answer immediately. His expression was bleak and his lips, set firmly, actually quivered. His gaze did not shift from Coppell's, who was glowering and whose eyes seemed buried deep in their sockets. The silence dragged on, the most surprising thing about it being that Coppell allowed it to last so long.

At last, Trannion placed his hands on the arm of his chair, and rose to his feet.

'Commander Coppell,' he said, 'I am from this moment resigning from the Metropolitan Police Force. In my written resignation which I shall send to the Assistant Commissioner and the Commissioner, I shall state that in thirty years of service to the Force I have never been submitted to such intolerable rudeness as in the past few minutes. I am not a young or inexperienced man who can be frightened by bullying or will submit to any form of tyranny.'

He bowed, stiffly, and turned to the door. He could not know that Coppell had never been so astounded in his life, and had actually opened the door before Coppell called out in a grating voice: 'Come back – please.' He seemed to choke. 'I'm sorry if I offended you.'

3

Orders

CHIEF SUPERINTENDENT MATTHEW Trannion seemed to hesitate, as if doubtful whether he should accept the apology and turn back. Coppell sat with his fingers gripping his chair-arms like vices. He looked as if he could spring up from his chair and leap at Trannion.

The silvery-haired man closed the door, slowly, and turned round. They eyed each other as if aware of each other for the first time, and then Coppell said: 'We'd better start again.'

Trannion sat down, saying: 'That is the wisest thing to do, sir.'

'We know the situation up to the time you finished the report and outlined the attitudes of the other four officers. Do you think any of them would talk about the case?'

'I would be extremely surprised, sir,' Trannion said. 'I most certainly would not.'

'Did they go back to their Divisions?'

'Yes, sir.'

'Was there any other evidence, beyond the scar, submitted at the meeting?'

'No.'

26

'How many had actually seen that scar on West's chin?'

'Only Partridge, sir – the others hadn't noticed it.'

'Well, the quicker we check whether it exists, the better,' Coppell said. 'Who would know?' He did not wait for an answer but said: 'It might be in his dossier. We don't want any alarm about this but we'll need his dossier if he's being considered for promotion.' He hesitated, and then went on: 'I'll check it myself. Where is West, do you know?'

'Having the day off, sir.'

'Humph. All right. I may need you again tonight.'

'I am at your disposal, sir. In fact I would like to spend some time with *Fingerprints* and *Ballistics* about some cases we've had lately – I'll be in one place or the other.'

Coppell nodded: 'Right.'

'Thank you,' replied Trannion, and went out.

For some moments Coppell stared at the door; then he began to glower, but suddenly be broke into a guffaw of laughter, thinking: I didn't know the old goat had it in him. He snorted two or three times as he pulled his telephone towards him and called the Secretary's Department, where staff records were kept. The man at the other end raised no demur when he asked for Roger West's file to be sent along at once. That would mean in about fifteen minutes' time. He made a few salient notes about what Trannion had told him and then telephoned the Assistant Commissioner for Crime.

'I'm sorry but he won't be back today,' a secretary told him.

'I'll call him in the morning,' Coppell said, glad that she couldn't see his broad grin, for this meant that he would have to talk to the Commissioner himself, for he could not allow the matter to wait overnight, and he had little time for the A.C. Moreover the Commissioner, Sir Jacob Trevillion, knew West, for they had once come into conflict much as he had, just now, with Trannion. Trevillion was a big, bluff, bucolic man, ex-navy with an admiral's rank, capable of putting the fear of God into ninety-nine men out of a hundred. Even now as he called him on the inter-office telephone, Coppell felt a little apprehensive – and the apprehension leapt sky-high when Trevillion himself barked:

'Commissioner!'

'This is Coppell, sir, Commander—'

'What is it, Coppell?'

'I would very much like to come and discuss an important matter with you.'

'Why me? Where's Mr Renfrew?'

'He's not in, sir.'

'And this is vital?'

'I think you'll agree that it is, sir.'

Trevillion said something which sounded like:'Better be,' and then called out to his secretary: 'Mavis! What time are the Scott-Gordons due... Well, give 'em a drink, tell them I'll be there as soon as I can... Coppell?' Coppell was treated to the full blast of the Admiral's bridge voice. 'I'll come to you, right away.'

He rang off before Coppell could make any comment.

He sat back for a moment, eased his collar, then sprang up and went to his washroom, washed his hands and face and combed his thick and wiry black hair, then wondered whether he should offer Trevillion a drink. He decided that this was a serious occasion, and drinks might give it too social and frivolous a touch. A tap at the door startled him and he called 'come in'. It was the messenger from the Secretary's Department with West's file.

'Put it on the desk,' growled Coppell.

'If you would just sign the receipt for it, sir.'

Coppell signed a slip of paper and thrust it back into the man's hand, then, as the door closed, pulled the file towards him. As always, photographs were kept in a pocket stuck on the inside of the stiff manilla folder, and he was taking these out when footsteps thumped along the passage and, without even a perfunctory tap, Sir Jacob Trevillion opened the door. Coppell saw a big, heavy-jowled man, almost aggressively healthy. Energy, and a harmless irascibility, seemed to spark from him.

'Thank you for coming, sir.' Coppell pushed a chair into position.

'Hope it won't take long,' said the Commissioner, facing Coppell and looking at him intently. 'I've two guests.' He snorted. 'Guests! Two friends of the Home Secretary's whose fool of a son lost a fortune at Black's two or three nights ago and they say he was robbed. Coppell, answer me this.'

'If I can.'

'I don't ask questions a man can't answer,' Trevillion growled; but there was a glint of humour in his eyes. 'Do you feel like throwing your hand in when I pressure you on something you're already doing your damnedest on?'

Coppell, taken by surprise by the unexpected question, pursed his lips in doubt, and then said: 'I want to keep my job too badly, sir. So the answer is "no".'

'What *do* you feel like?'

Coppell was surprised into a laugh.

'Well, like the chap who was in here only half-an-hour or so ago, although he *did* threaten to throw his hand in. He told me where to get off.'

'Know what you mean,' said Trevillion. 'Like to know something, Coppell? I still haven't sorted out the difference between discipline in the navy and in the police.' There was hardly a pause before he changed the subject, beginning with a kind of bark. 'Well – what's the trouble? This invisible chap?'

'Er – in a way, sir. *Yes,* sir.'

'So your chaps found out something. About time.'

'I don't know whether they have or not but I'm sure you ought to know. Care to look at these, sir?' Coppell went on. He turned to his desk, selected a photograph of West, a portrait showing him as he had been ten years or so ago, and an enlargement of the photograph Alice Brace had sent out. He placed them side by side.

Trevillion stared down; moved to one side; shifted the pictures at different angles, and then barked: 'Well?'

'The committee of five superintendents say that although it doesn't show in this photograph - and I've checked and it doesn't show in any, sir - West has a scar like that one –' he pointed '– under his chin.'

Trevillion did not speak until he had looked at the photographs again for several minutes. Then he said: 'Knives out for West. Hey?'

'Nothing vindictive in this, sir.'

'Yes. They're bloody unhappy at the thought.'

'So am I, sir. In the little time I've had to think, sir – *very* unhappy. It's nonsense, of course.'

'Why?'

Coppell eased his collar. This was a moment when he desperately needed a drink.

'Well, dammit, you must have some reasons,' growled Trevillion, and looked about him. 'Do you keep whisky in here?'

'I do, sir.'

'Past my usual time,' stated Trevillion, and watched as Coppell went to a cupboard and took out Johnnie Walker, a soda syphon and glasses. He poured the drinks, stopping at Trevillion's "Whoa!" and took a gulp gratefully. 'In the first place the girl who sent this out had time to write on the back but didn't mention West.'

'Good point. Go on.'

'For a second, only a few months ago West turned down a job which could have given him a life of luxury, because he preferred the Yard.'

Trevillion nodded and sipped.

'Good *prima facie* that he has no motive. Next?'

'It just isn't West, sir.'

'Very poor reason for a policeman,' barked Trevillion.

'Best reason there is,' retorted Coppell. 'Got to know your men – and I know West.'

He eyed the older man straightly but not in defiance, and they both sipped again before Trevillion said: 'We want a picture of West lying down in much the same position.'

'They're not two a penny, sir.'

'Wasn't there one when he was caught with that woman with photographers who—'

'No, sir.'

'Humph. Pity.' Trevillion brooded. 'Home.'

Coppell was startled. 'What about home, sir? If you're ready to go—'

'*West's* home. Should be plenty of pictures there, romping with his family – hey! Gymnasium.'

'I hadn't thought about that, sir.'

'Well, think now. And if there's nothing in the Yard's sporting archives, we need to look at the photo albums he keeps at home.'

Coppell drained his glass to the last drop, and then asked curiously: 'With or without his knowledge?'

'Without, if we can.'

Coppell said: 'Oh, hell. If it's got to be done we could do it tonight. He's taking his wife out to dinner, and they went to a matinée this afternoon. And one of his sons is in Australia and the other's on a television film location in India, so the house is empty. But I don't like it.'

'Of course you don't like it,' said Trevillion. 'Got to do it, though. Who will you use?'

Coppell pondered for a long time, and then said: 'I'll go myself. If I give the job to someone else word might get out, and – I'll go myself,' he repeated.

'How will you get in?'

'Another whisky before you go?' Coppell avoided the question.

'No, must fly,' said Trevillion. 'Call me at home when you have the results.'

'Right.' Coppell nodded. 'If he *has* that scar, sir, I'd want to tell him what's on.'

'Use your own judgment,' conceded the Commissioner, and he went off, slamming the door behind him.

Coppell poured himself another drink, and then went moodily to the desk and studied the two photographs. The man in bed was older and the angle of the face was different, but they looked as alike as two peas.

'I hope to God he hasn't got that scar,' Coppell said, and downed the rest of his drink.

4

Search

COPPELL TURNED OUT of busy King's Road, Chelsea, into Bell Street, where the Wests lived. Built between the wars the houses on either side were very different from one another; red brick might stand by stucco, yellow brick by stone from Bath or Portland; two were even of the Swiss chalet style. Since the houses were solid and well-maintained, for most of the people in Bell Street were in the higher-middle income group, and the gardens were matured and well cared for, the whole street gave pleasure.

Forsythia and flowering cherry, flowering currant, may trees and may hedges, all of these and other ornamental bushes were blooming, while in the middle of one green lawn which looked as smooth as a billiard table, was a single magnolia tree. The late spring had delayed growth, but three nights without frost had allowed the blooms to come out to such perfection that all those who passed paused to enjoy and admire.

Coppell saw half-a-dozen people outside this magnolia house, which was a few doors away from the Wests but on the other side of the street. He parked his car outside the Wests' garage, the door of which stood open, and went boldly to the front door. Years ago there had been danger here for Janet West, and Coppell had given several of the men on duty near the house keys, so that in emergency they could get in. One of these keys had been in Coppell's desk for so long that he remembered it only when rummaging for papers pushed to the back.

Now, he took it from his pocket.

Of course, West might have had his lock changed, in which case the back door might be the best way in. Coppell inserted the key, and turned; the lock yielded, the door opened at a touch.

He stepped inside, closed the door, and listened; then in a low-pitched but carrying voice he called: 'Anyone at home?' There was no answer. From that moment Coppell behaved exactly like the policeman he had been trained to be: quick, quiet, efficient – and well-prepared. The first and most obvious place for a photograph album was the front or living-room, where he had been occasionally. He went in. The daylight was still quite good enough to see by. Over on a sideboard he noticed the unmistakable back of a photograph album.

Luck, first try?

He stepped across, opened, and thumbed through it – and soon grimaced with disappointment, for this was of the Wests' children, Martin and Richard. Coppell snapped his fingers in exasperation. There was not a single family portrait, just of the children – from naked-on-a-couch stage to strapping young men in boxing gloves or swimming trunks; a nice-looking pair. He closed the album, and began to look round, and almost immediately saw another album on the shelf of a rather battered bookcase. It passed through Coppell's mind that this room hadn't been refurnished in over twenty-five years. West didn't exactly make a fortune out of his graft – if graft it was!

Coppell chuckled.

'Bloody nonsense,' he said aloud.

There were a few photographs of Roger and Janet from their wedding day onwards and some formal family groups, but nothing to give Coppell what he wanted. The 'happy snaps' of this family were obviously kept in another room.

He ran through the drawers of tables and a chest in a room next to the kitchen, but no snapshots.

He went up the stairs.

There were four bedrooms and one bathroom, and he knew that West and his wife slept in the front room.

He stepped in.

There was the big, old-fashioned bedstead with handsome wooden head and foot panels, a Victorian wardrobe which took up the whole of one wall. '*Graft!*' Coppell grunted half-sneering, and then began to look for photographs.

There were one or two informal family groups standing about.

There was a tall chest of drawers with a small mirror standing on top, and he opened the top drawer to find gloves, handkerchiefs, oddments; those underneath contained folded slips, stockings, and – *photographs*. There must be fifty of them, and as he looked at them Coppell saw they were mostly of Roger – with cricket, football and swimming teams, actually at judo and karate classes. Now and again he was on his back, in others his head was tilted backwards. Coppell saw enough to be sure that he had to look at these more carefully, through a magnifying glass if necessary, and he gathered them up in his arms and turned towards the door.

A man flew at him from the open doorway.

He had no time to see more than that he was solid and big but not tall; and that his face was set and his eyes blazing. Coppell dropped the books and kicked out – but the other man grabbed his ankle and heaved him backwards; he went flying onto the bed, quite helpless and so twisted that he couldn't see round at his assailant.

He felt a powerful hand at his wrist; felt his arms thrust up behind him in a hammer-lock, pain at elbow and shoulder so excruciating that he cried out.

'Just make one move and I'll break your arm,' the man said.

Coppell had a feeling that he would do exactly that.

'Now wriggle round so that you're face downwards on the bed.'

Coppell hesitated for a moment, and then felt the other's grip slacken enough to allow him to obey without giving himself too much pain. Very slowly he worked his body round until suddenly the other ordered: 'Wait.'

Coppell stopped.

Still keeping his hold, the other did an astonishing thing: he pulled the laces of Coppell's shoes until they loosened, and then ordered:

'Kick your shoes off.'

For the first time Coppell hesitated.

'But why should – *ach*!'

The other pushed his arm further up and there was a flash of pain. So Coppell kicked his shoes off and they fell, each with a heavy clump, onto the floor. Without waiting to be told, Coppell moved so that he was face downwards on the bed, head turned to one side to avoid being smothered, left arm still pushed up behind his back so that movement hurt.

'Now,' the man said. 'Who are you?'

'I warn you—' began Coppell, and then gasped: '*Ach*! You're breaking my arm.'

'And your neck if you don't answer my questions,' the other said. 'Who are you?'

There was no way of giving an answer; and no way of living this down if it reached the Press, or even spread throughout the Yard. Coppell knew that and felt the remorseless increasing of the pressure at his arm, and yet he hated to have to answer.

The man said: 'I shall ask you once more before I break your arm.' He did not ask the question immediately, Coppell actually had time to wonder who would be watching West's house; and to reflect also that this man was young, remarkably strong, and had a deep, educated voice.

Now, with great deliberation, he asked: 'Who – are – you?'

Coppell said: 'I am a senior detective officer from Scotland Yard and my name is Coppell – Frank Coppell.'

He felt the hold relax.

He sensed that the other was so astounded that for a vital moment he would be vulnerable. Coppell snatched his arm from the other's grasp, twisted round and kicked out, remembering suddenly that he had no shoes. He saw the other draw back, as he sprang to a standing position.

He saw a rage-filled, handsome face.

He saw a clenched fist coming at him which he had no time to dodge; the blow caught him on the side of

the jaw and he went down as if made of crumbling
lead. His head struck a corner of the bedside table and
he lost consciousness.

And yet – consciousness did not go altogether.

He saw against the darkness a glimmer of light and
had awareness of movement and of his head being
touched. Soon, he realised that his attacker was ex-
amining the spot where it had struck the table. The
other straightened up, and moved away, but didn't go
far; he sat on the side of the bed, looking downwards,
for perhaps five minutes Then he disappeared, only to
return with a glass of water. He went down on one
knee, raising Coppell's head, and put the glass to his
lips.

Gratefully, Coppell sipped. The other put the glass
to one side and asked:

'Can you get up?'

'I daresay.'

'I'll give you a hand.'

A 'hand' proved to be the support of a very strong
arm, and even with it Coppell had difficulty in getting
halfway to his feet so that he could drop onto the bed.
That had been a punch in a thousand; what a boxer
called a 'killer punch' and delivered to the right spot
there was no doubt at all, it could kill. Even now his
head swam and he could not focus his gaze properly.

The other man said: 'So you're Commander
Coppell.'

He hadn't called himself 'Commander' but he
answered: 'Yes.'

'I'm Martin West.'

'*What?*' gasped Coppell, and so jarred his head that
he actually pressed his palms against his ears to try to
calm the sound. He knew he said but did not hear

himself saying: 'I thought you were in Australia.'

'I was, until three days ago.'

'Have you been in the house all the time?'

'No. I was across the street looking at the magnolia tree when I saw you come in. What are you doing here?' His expression hardened again and he looked dangerously aggressive.

Coppell said reasoningly: 'Martin, don't you think you would be wise to wait until—'

'Don't "Martin" me, Commander. And no, I don't think it would be wise to wait. I want to know what you're doing here and I want to know now. Just in case you've forgotten, you forced your way into this house. You've no right here, and you've a damned sight less right to go hunting through my mother's clothes and my father's private papers. And I'm so flaming mad I would break your arm or your neck as soon as look at you. Let's have it – what are you doing here?'

This 'boy', thought Coppell, was in his late twenties. He was an artist who had hoped to make a living in Australia, but it didn't matter what had brought him back. He was a son of Roger West, and he meant exactly what he said. That was a streak of ruthlessness in him as there was in West – as there had to be in all good policemen. At this moment the muscles of his hands and jaw were flexing; no doubt his whole body was; and God knew what tricks of karate and judo he might know.

'I came to look for a particular photograph of your father,' he said.

'Why not ask him for it?'

'I didn't want him to know I was looking.'

'Afraid *he* might break your neck, too?'

'No,' Coppell said, and was suddenly surprised by

his own restraint; the fact that he did not actually feel like knocking West across the room. He wanted to be conciliatory not simply to get himself out of an awkward situation but to help the boy. Boy! 'No, I'm not afraid of your father breaking my neck although he's often wanted to. If I could find the photograph I'm looking for it might clear up a peculiar situation which has arisen at the Yard.'

The younger man began to frown, and when he spoke it was in a more subdued voice.

'You mean, he's under suspicion.'

'I don't think so, yet. That's why I came here myself. If I could clear the thing up without having to talk to others it would be better all round.'

Martin West said slowly: 'That was decent of you.'

Coppell didn't reply. Though a little late for his comfort, he knew that he now had Martin with him, there would be no more conflict if he handled the situation well, and he felt in his bones that he was doing so.

'One other thing,' Martin went on. 'If you'd found what you wanted, could you have avoided telling my father?'

'I think so. I would try to. It would be impossible if I – if I didn't get what I wanted from here.'

'What *do* you want, exactly?'

'A photograph like this – not the same one, it was taken only a few days ago, but one showing your father's head in about the same position.' The implication in the photograph was clear, the man in the bed was waiting for a woman to join him. How would this son, so fiercely proud of his father, react to the obvious? Would he suffer an emotional storm, of anger, resentment, repugnance? There was no way of telling.

He handed the enlargement of Alice Brace's snapshot to Martin, who turned it round slowly, frowning. There was no indication that he was going to be outraged or insulted.

'How long ago, then, was it taken?' he asked.

'We think, last Monday.' It was Wednesday now. 'It reached us as a snapshot on Tuesday by the morning post, and was taken by a police officer working on a very rough case.' He paused long enough to allow Martin to absorb all this, and went on: 'The woman police officer was murdered and thrown into the Thames where she was found early this morning.'

For the first time Martin's eyes flared up.

'You suspect him of *murder*?'

'If he's the man of the photograph, yes, we suspect him of murder and a lot of other things,' Coppell answered calmly. 'That's why I want a certain photograph which shows his face, particularly his chin, from that angle.'

There was a long, tense silence.

It was impossible to imagine what the other was thinking, and Coppell didn't try; but it was easy to imagine what he was feeling: fear, dread, perhaps even despair.

Then, in a husky voice, Martin asked: 'Why is a similar photograph so important?'

'Because this one –' Coppell pointed to the one still in Martin's hand '– has a distinguishing mark on the chin, a small scar which normally doesn't show because it's underneath, but is particularly noticeable in this one, probably because of a trick of the light. Do you see the scar?'

Martin stared down at it, and Coppell began to have a strange, cold, near frightening feeling. The boy's reaction was not at all what he had expected; and there was no possible doubt now of the fear in those bright grey eyes.

'Yes, I see the scar,' he said. 'Dad has one, just there. But—' He gulped, and seemed to have great difficulty in speaking. 'You'll think I'm just saying this so as to - to defend my father. But I'm not. That's the scar all right and in the same place but that's *not* a photograph of my father.'

5

Reunion

COPPELL THOUGHT WITH a kind of distress very rare in him: what else can he say? He watched the strong, broad face, the slightly crooked nose, the sensitive, well-shaped lips. The last words had brought fresh tension into the room and Coppell wanted to find a way of breaking it. He said almost the first thing that came into his head.

'Can you be sure?'

'I *am* sure.'

'Can you prove it?'

Martin said: 'It doesn't need proof. It isn't my father.'

'Martin,' Coppell said, 'there is just about one way of finding out for certain. That is by having a photograph taken of your father in that position. As there's no doubt about the scar I have to take the matter up much further – you see that, don't you?'

'Yes,' Martin answered shortly.

'And it would be much better for me to talk to him, or one of his associates at the Yard. That way your mother wouldn't have to know—' Coppell faltered. 'Well at least she wouldn't have to know the compromising nature of the picture.'

Martin looked at him very steadily for a long time,

frowning. His face did not clear as he replied in a voice which he kept level and unemotional only with a great effort:

'So I just say nothing, is that what you mean? I come home unexpectedly from Australia, and they kill the fatted calf, and I jump for joy and pretend I don't know that in the morning my father is going to run into this blockbuster and for all they know you'll prove what isn't true and smash their lives. Oh, that's going to be easy for me, the dutiful son, isn't it? Kiss Mum, shake hands with Dad, tell them how wonderful they look, say how glad I am to be back home, how are tricks at the Yard, Pop, what's your latest triumph? You see how easy it would be, Commander. Well, let's have one thing crystal clear: *I* tell him. *I* show him that photograph. *He* decides whether to let Mother see it or not. Not you, the A.C., the Commissioner or any of you who aren't worth—' He gulped. 'Or anyone else. Have you any idea where they are?'

'They're out at dinner.'

'Then they won't be too late. May I have this photograph? Or will you send another?'

Coppell hesitated. 'You can keep that one.'

'Thanks.' Martin looked back at him speculatively. 'I'll make a deal with you, Commander.'

'What deal?'

'You accept my right to help my father as much as I can in this case, and I'll tell him you called here to see him and I managed to persuade you to tell me what it was all about. That way he needn't know about your snooping or about our fight. *That's* fair enough, isn't it?'

Coppell answered: 'Yes.' But his voice was guarded. There was obviously something which lay very heavily on his mind, although he couldn't bring himself to say it. But at last he did, moving across to a chair and sinking into it as if he were physically weary.

'You could help us, too.'

'You mean, against my father?'

'In a way, yes.'

'You must be off your head.'

'Didn't he teach you to listen before making up your mind about anything?' asked Coppell, and won first a blank stare and then a slow, amused smile from the younger man.

'Yes. Go ahead.'

'There is one way in which he could be involved.' Martin didn't break in with a hot denial, so Coppell went on: 'He could be deliberately involved. He was, once before: he joined a gang of criminals so that he could work against them from the inside. You probably aren't old enough to remember the case, but—'

'I've heard the story,' Martin interrupted, and nodded: 'I suppose it's possible this time.' He gave a humourless smile and went on: 'Okay, I'll try to find that out.'

'Without letting him know what you're doing?'

'I won't tell him unless it's unavoidable,' Martin promised.

'I can't ask for more than that,' Coppell said, getting slowly to his feet. 'I'll be on my way then.' He added drily: 'I suppose I ought to be grateful that you didn't break my arm.'

Martin gave a rather shamefaced grin, as he turned and went downstairs ahead of Coppell. Across the road at least twenty people were standing and staring at the magnolia tree, and a policeman was on duty, moving traffic on and keeping the pedestrians to the path. No one appeared to take any notice of Coppell or Martin, who turned slowly back to the house, went inside, and closed the door quietly. Then he let out a long, slow breath which grew into a whistle and as he walked towards the stairs, he muttered: 'How I wish old Richard were here!'

Well, Richard was not there, nor was he likely to be home for several weeks. The burden of trying to help his father rested solely on himself.

He carried the athletic and sporting pictures back to the drawer, tidied the bed, straightened two or three chairs, and then went slowly to the table where the photograph lay. He looked at it hard and long, and could almost hear the echo of his own voice, saying: 'That's not a photograph of my father.'

But already doubt had begun to creep in.

It was remarkably like him. He could remember coming into the room one morning he had been very young, and seeing his father like that. He could remember his father calling in his deep, happy voice:

'Come on, old chap!'

And he had raced towards the outstretched arms and leapt into them, been held tight and lifted high and then turned towards his mother, who smiled back at him. It had been a golden moment and there had been many of them, especially in his early days: five, six, seven years old.

That photograph could not be of his father.

He wondered where they had gone and how late they would be. The recent letters, mostly from his mother, had said they were going out together more, that Roger wasn't under so much pressure, and they could now afford. . .

That photograph could not be of his father.

He went into his own room, where Coppell would have seen a battered suitcase and a hold-all, a folding easel, a few unframed paintings; part of his work in Australia, which had hardly been a brilliant success. He unpacked a few things, and then began to go downstairs. He was only halfway down when a key was inserted in the front door, although it couldn't be nine o'clock. What were they doing home so early? *Had someone told them of the photograph?* He had to fight against that thought, had to look as if he hadn't a thought in the world except for them. And they would be astounded! He had meant to call from Rome, and failed; and there had been no answer when he had called from Heathrow. He stood a few steps up from the hall, just standing and smiling, and wondering who would see him first.

The front door opened and a girl appeared: a complete stranger. His grin froze on his face, and he gaped in astonishment. At any other time he would have been intrigued by the girl, who was slim and rather attractive, with light hair and a fair complexion. She stood in the doorway, her hand on the key, staring, as astounded as he. Beyond was the street with passing people; cars, the trees, dusk, street lights already on.

She drew back a pace.

'Who—' she began.

'*Who?*' he demanded.

'What are you doing here?' Her voice rose. 'Don't come nearer or I'll scream for help.'

'*You'll* scream for help!' he gulped. 'From the police, I presume?'

'Yes,' she replied, sharply, 'and don't think I won't. There's one outside.'

'There will soon be one inside, too,' he said, and went down a step, but obviously she was stiff with fright, and she not only backed a pace but looked round as if to run. So he schooled himself to go on in a much calmer voice: 'There must be some kind of mistake.'

'*I* haven't made a mistake. I live here.'

This girl? Living here? That was utter nonsense, and she couldn't possibly expect him to believe it. And then suddenly there was a change in her expression, the fear seemed to die away, something like laughter showed in her eyes.

'You're *Martin*!' she exclaimed.

'Well, you haven't made a mistake about that, anyhow,' he conceded. 'I wish I knew who you are. I've only been away three years so you can't be a sister no one told me about.'

'Ass,' she said. 'I'm just a – friend.'

'Who lives here.'

'Yes. You see, my parents had to move to South Africa in a hurry, Daddy's a civil engineer and something went wrong with a bridge over the Zambesi or some other river—'

'The Limpopo,' Martin suggested.

Her eyes lit up. 'That's it! The Limpopo! How on earth did you know?'

'A bridge fell down into the Limpopo River a few weeks ago,' Martin answered, 'so it seemed probable. How – er – how long have you lived here?'

'A month.'

'And it's a month since I left Port Darwin,' he said. 'I haven't had any letters.' Now he walked down the stairs and she closed the door behind her and came towards him. 'I suppose I should know your name.'

'Oh, yes! Anne.'

'Boleyn?'

She laughed. 'Anne Claire.' She drew a deep breath. 'My, you'll get it from your mother when she arrives home.'

'Oh,' Martin said. He spoke in a softer, more diffident manner, although there was nothing diffident about what he said. 'I'd rather hoped she might be pleased but you've known her more recently than I have.'

'She'll whoop for joy! But she hasn't heard from you for six weeks and she's not at all sure you haven't been eaten by man-eating tigers.'

'Now hold it,' Martin interrupted. 'Kangaroos and koala bears don't eat would-be artists, nor do dingoes unless very provoked. The biggest danger in Australia comes from snakes, and they are fairly fastidious, too.' He laughed. 'Mother will be all right once she's over the shock. As I hope you will be.'

'Well so far I like what I've seen of you,' declared Anne with refreshing candour. 'But you were the last thing I expected to see. Have you had dinner?'

'No.'

'Why don't you let me cook you something?' suggested Anne.

'You mean my mother allows you the freedom of her kitchen?' Martin said faintly. 'This isn't simply going to surprise her, it is going to kill me. I—'

He broke off.

He did not know what it was that brought Coppell's visit so vividly to mind; what made him see a vision of the photograph, which was still upstairs in the main bedroom. He must get it away or there would be alarm the moment either of his parents entered. He did not know, either, what a change it made in his expression, but he did see alarm suddenly chase contentment across hers, and tension was with them again.

'What is it?' Anne demanded.

'I – ah – I just remembered a message I have to give them and I'm not very happy about it,' answered Martin, 'and it's nothing I can discuss with you, I'm afraid. I'm sorry—'

'There isn't the slightest need to be sorry! But do come and have supper. Would bacon and eggs be all right?'

'Perfect!'

'And there are some potatoes I can fry,' Anne went on. 'Why don't you have a wash while I get supper, and then I'll go up to my room – Richard's really – and watch television or read until you've had your confidential talk with your parents.'

He did as she suggested. She cooked bacon and eggs and her fried potatoes were crisp and flavourful. They washed up together, and by that time it was after nine o'clock. Martin went to the foot of the stairs with her, and quite suddenly she gripped his hands tightly, looking up into his face with a raking, searching glance.

'You aren't going to hurt them, are you? You haven't – haven't come home in disgrace?'

Across her words came the sound of a car engine and a moment later light from headlamps shone momentarily through the glass of the front door as Roger West turned his car into the garage, only a few feet away.

Anne pulled herself free and ran upstairs, calling: 'They needn't know I'm home!'

He heard her door – Richard's door – close quietly, heard the sounds which always came from the garage, but not his mother's footsteps. So they were coming in together, after locking the garage doors. His heart began to beat fast; painfully. His surprise arrival would have been enough to cope with, but there was the awful business of the photograph.

He rememberd he had left it, face upwards, on the sideboard.

He ran in, flipped it over, changed his mind and slid it between the pages of a family photograph album, and went back to the hall. As he reached it the door opened and his mother stepped in, with his father only a step behind her.

6

Joy to Anger

JANET STOPPED IN her tracks.

She looked beautiful; her face slightly flushed, her
eyes round with surprise. She stared at Martin – *damn
that photograph!* – and the colour seemed to ebb from
her cheeks. Roger West, coming up behind her, looked
over her shoulder.

'*Martin!*'

Janet still did not move; it was as if she were in a
trance. She stared into Martin's eyes, searching, prob-
ing, as if she could not really believe what she saw.
Then with a curious little sound, half-sob, half-cry, she
flung herself forward, and he enfolded her in a bear
hug which drove the breath out of her body. She
looked up at him, pale, tense, still only half-believing.

'Oh, Martin,' she said, huskily. 'Martin.'

There was a lump in Martin's throat as he forced
himself to say: 'You mean you haven't forgotten me?'

'*Martin!*' Roger West said again, in a deep voice
which had an edge to it.

Martin freed his right hand, and gripped his
father's. They stood like that for a few moments, and
then Janet put her face up to be kissed, brushing his lips
with her own.

'Why on earth didn't you let us know?'

Martin gave a sheepish grin. 'Well, you know me. Lowest ever on organisation. As a matter of fact—'

'Oh, it doesn't really matter,' Janet decided, 'you're here. Oh my dear, how I've longed to see you! How long have you been here? Did you get yourself anything to eat? How are you – you haven't come home because you're ill, have you? You haven't picked up some dreadful disease over there?'

Martin grinned, counting solemnly on each finger. 'Two hours. . . Yes, I'm fed. . . No, I haven't got the plague or anything serious I know of. I just—' He moved forward and lifted her off the ground, whirling her round before putting her down again. 'Where did you get the elixir?'

'What on earth are you talking about?'

'The elixir which makes you grow younger.'

'Now *that* sounds more like Richard – Richard isn't here, is he?'

'I haven't seen him. Isn't he supposed to be televising the Arabs in Timbuctoo or somewhere?'

Janet took off her hat and ran her fingers through her dark hair, then unbuttoned her coat. Beneath, she wore a simple sheath dress of primrose yellow. 'If I'd dreamt you'd be home I shouldn't have set foot outside the door.'

'There's gratitude for you,' Martin said, with a wink at his father. 'I'll bet you've been nagging Dad to take you out for weeks.'

'Months,' corrected Roger.

Janet turned to him and slid an arm through his, then one through Martin's, and – Janet in the lead, the men slightly behind because of the narrowness of the passage – they went into the living-room, where Janet placed her coat over a chair, raised her face and said: 'I

sense eggs and bacon – are you sure you had enough?'
And then: 'At least we'll have some coffee, or would
you two rather have a beer?'

'Coffee for me,' Martin said.

'I've had all I can drink tonight,' Roger assured her.

'Then I'll put the coffee on and then run upstairs
and tidy up.'

Both of them knew that this was one of her discerning moments; that she realised father and son needed
a few minutes on their own together and was making it
easy for them. She moved with unstudied grace about
the kitchen, putting water in the percolator, measuring the coffee, plugging in the pot. Then she said: 'You
can put the cups out,' and gave Martin a little,
breathless hug, reached the door, and then spun
round, alarm on her face.

'Martin!' It was always 'Martin!' in times of stress or
crisis.

'Yes, mother dear?'

'You're not going away again right away, are you?'

'Not for several weeks, at the very earliest.'

'Thank goodness for that,' she said, and turned and
hurried along the passage by the stairs, then up them;
her footsteps were feather-light, and ceased altogether
when she went into the main bedroom. Both men
smiled with warmth and affection, feeling her presence
still hovering about the room. Then Roger took the
initiative.

'You look fine,' he said. 'What brought you back?'

Martin said: 'I suppose it was homesickness as much
as anything. Mind you, I don't think I would have felt
so homesick if I'd done better.'

'No luck at all?' asked Roger.

'Oh, I sold a few paintings but if I hadn't picked up

odd jobs – I was a postman for three months and in a bookshop for six! – I couldn't have got by. I – er – well I thought Australia would bring out all that's best in my work, but instead it made me wonder if there *is* any best.'

'And you're going to find out here?'

'Yes,' Martin answered. 'I've decided that if I can't break through at least enough to make a living in England I'd better try something else. I'd been thinking like this for a long time, and then I got a chance to work my passage on an old tramp steamer coming from Brisbane to Rome, of all places. Then I found there was a cruise ship in Naples which wanted dining-room stewards – and here I am!'

Roger chuckled.

'It sounds quite a trip!' He eyed his son thoughtfully for some moments, and then asked:

'No trouble?'

'No, Dad. Why?'

'Then what's on your mind?' Roger demanded.

'Oh, lord,' breathed Martin. 'Does it show as plainly as that?'

'Yes. Are you planning to get married, or is there a girl who—'

'Good God, no!' Martin burst out with such vehemence that his father laughed. The silence which followed seemed not only deep but profound. There was a footstep upstairs – Janet might be coming down at any moment and if anything was certain it was that he had to tell his father about the photograph and Coppell while they were alone. No footsteps sounded on the landing or the stairs, however, and Roger put a hand lightly on his son's arm and said: 'Tell me, old boy.'

'It's nothing directly to do with me,' Martin said.

'Mysteriouser and mysteriouser!' Roger said lightly.

'Dad – I'm as worried as hell.'

'Yes, I can see that. Don't pull any punches. Tell me.'

Roger watched as Martin drew a deep breath, and using as few words as he could, explained what had happened, and about what he had told Coppell. All the time his eyes, burning, were studying his father's handsome face, a face he seemed to be seeing for the first time tonight: stern; drawn; jaw and lips set. Not once during the narration did he interrupt; but twice he fingered the scar beneath his chin.

At last, Martin finished, saying miserably: 'Ever since I told him about the scar I could have kicked myself.'

'Nonsense. You would have been a fool not to. In any case – Coppell didn't really come for a photograph, he came to look at the house and find out if there was any evidence that I'd been throwing money about lately – evidence of any kind. Let's go and see that pretty picture.'

He led the way into the dining-room, and Martin took the picture out of the album. Roger studied it, pursing his lips. It seemed a long time before he put it down. Then he said mildly: 'One thing you have to get absolutely clear in your mind, Martin.'

'What's that?'

'That is *not* me.'

Martin muttered, relief so great that he tried to hide it: 'I knew it couldn't be, and yet it was so damnably like you I even found myself wondering. Dad, I'm sorry—'

'Martin, it's a long time since you and I agreed we

wouldn't be sorry about telling the truth.' Unexpectedly, Roger burst into a chuckle. 'I'll tell you one thing. Your mother will swear it's me when she first sees it. I think we'd better keep this from her until the morning.'

At that moment, they heard a sound, as of a catch of breath, at the door. They spun round. Janet wasn't in sight, but there was no doubt she was outside. Roger went to the door and saw her at the foot of the stairs. She had put on a pale blue dressing-gown and taken a lot of trouble with her hair, but the radiance had gone from her face.

'Come in, Jan,' Roger said.

'It's all right,' she said, stiffly. 'If there's something you don't want to tell me, that's quite all right with me. I shouldn't have eavesdropped. I wouldn't have but I heard Martin say he was sorry, and—'

'You shall now hear why,' Roger said, 'even if it does mean a sleepless night.' He went forward, and putting his arms round her kissed her gently. 'Now come and pour out that coffee and listen.' He led the way, and Martin who had left home at a time when there had been some problems between his parents, followed, frowning. Soon they were sitting round the table in the room next to the kitchen. Roger switched on the record-player, filling the air with music, soft, symphonic, soothing. 'Now,' he repeated, 'take one look at this – I'll allow you ten seconds! – and tell me who it is.'

He handed her the photograph, face downwards. She flipped it over and then gasped:

'Why, it's—'

'*Ten seconds*!' roared Roger. 'Count up to ten, Martin.'

There were moments of startled silence before Martin began to count, slowly and deliberately. All the time Janet stared down at the photograph, gripping it tightly.

'... eight... nine... ten.' Martin finished.

'It's *you*!' cried Janet, her eyes flashing, her voice actually quivering with tension. 'It's you, and you must be waiting for.... Oh, what a horrible thing to happen, tonight of all nights.' She glared at Roger as he leaned towards her, then suddenly gripped the picture as if to rip it apart. Before she could start, Roger had it from her, and tossed it aside. She watched him, eyes bright, lips parted, colour mounting to her cheeks, her anger so great that she could hardly get the words out. 'It's an awful thing to show me, it's - it's like flaunting another woman in my face *and* in front of my son—'

'Jan,' Roger interrupted, 'you're behaving like a spoiled brat in a tantrum. Stop it.'

'You've the nerve to stand there and insult—'

'And you've the nerve to jump to the conclusion that the photograph's of me.'

'But it *is*.'

'You of all people ought to know better.'

'Now if you think a little blarney—'

'Martin,' said Roger, turning away as if he knew that it was impossible to reason with her, 'will you look up Commander Coppell's home telephone number, it's on the list stuck at the back of the telephone book, and ask him if I can come and see him right away – at his place or at the Yard, I don't mind where.'

Martin hesitated, as if to ask: 'Dad, are you sure?'

'What on earth has Coppell to do with this?' demanded Janet, her mood suddenly quieter.

'He had this sent to him as proof that I am a master

criminal,' Roger said, drily. 'I have somehow to convince him that I'm not. Martin happened to—'

'But it's ludicrous!'

'What is ludicrous?'

'Suspecting you of being a criminal!'

'A *master* criminal.'

'Any kind of criminal. The man must be mad.'

'He's not mad,' Roger replied quietly. 'He must have had good reasons for coming here and looking for photographs to compare with this one—'

'Coppell *here*?' She spun round on Martin. 'What on earth happened?'

'We had a bit of a do, actually.'

'Speak plain English! What is a bit of a do?'

'First, I gather, Martin nearly broke his arm, and then he nearly broke his neck, and finally they parted friends – except that Martin had to tell me about it tonight. You may or may not believe it but that photograph is a fake. It is not me. It is being used to involve me. I don't know who took it or who the man is but I'm going to find out.' He waited for a few seconds and then his voice quietened. 'I didn't want to spoil tonight for you, Jan, and nothing need have happened until the morning.'

Janet said in a mumbling voice: 'It *does* look like you. Why should you say I'm the one person who should know it's not?'

'I'll give you a clue,' Roger said, enormously relieved that the atmosphere was so much lighter. 'It was taken within the past forty-eight hours.'

'Well, *I* haven't been with you every minute of the last forty-eight,' Janet retorted tartly. 'It looks as if I should—'

'Oh, Mum,' Martin interrupted. 'Mum, *please*.'

7

Blow Hot, Blow Cold?

ROGER KNEW HIS wife perhaps better even than he knew himself. Knew her faults and failings; knew the moods of jealousy which could possess her, turning her into a shrew for a few dreadful minutes; at their worst, a few dreadful hours. But of late, because he had been able to spend more time at home because of a new form of work he had been given, only the best side had shown. The good, the adorable, the kind, the generous, the understanding. Of all the things that had happened on this strange night, perhaps the worst was to see how swiftly Janet had reverted to one of her old, savage, vitriolic moods; how thin was the line between good and bad, even now. Perhaps for the first time – although he had suspected it before – the demands of his work, the conditions of living, were not the causes for her moods. They were just Janet. And now, in or fast approaching the change of life, how much more likely it was that she would flare up out of calmness; how much more necessary to help her.

Now, a protest had been wrung from Martin who had seldom – virtually never – taken sides between them on any issue.

He watched the struggle going on in Janet, as he watched the pain growing in his son's eyes. Then to his enormous relief he saw Janet's face clear and heard her say: 'Give me another clue, then.'

Roger simply ran his hand over his forehead and thick, curly hair, and over the back of his neck to his jacket collar. Next, he smoothed the side of his face just below the temple. Martin watched with as much bewilderment as Janet, until a sudden enlightenment appeared on her face.

'You've had a haircut!'

'A week ago.'

'You were letting your hair grow too long.'

'Even Richard said so, before he left.'

'And—' Janet turned to the photograph, now in Roger's hand. '*He* hasn't had a haircut.'

'Dad,' protested Martin in an astonished voice, 'surely you didn't let your hair grow as long as that!'

'Nearly.'

'After all you've said about mine!'

'Yours was deliberate, mine was finding time,' Roger said. He slid his arm about Janet's shoulders and placed the photograph on the table, then said to Martin: 'There's the newspaper clippings book over there behind the sewing machine. Fetch it, will you?' They waited as Martin went across to a shelf above the sewing machine; lying flat on this were several big Press cuttings books, and Roger added: 'The top one.' Martin brought it over and placed it on the table then opened it to a recently filled page. There was a head and shoulders portrait of him as he peered up at a window where thieves had broken in the previous night. The angle of this picture was remarkably like the one in the picture sent by Police Officer Alice Brace, and it showed him before his haircut.

'Dad,' Martin said in a strained voice.

'Yes.'

'This hair is *longer* and more curly than the man's on the bed. Especially at the back of the neck. Chaps at school used to say you had your hair curled at a hairdresser's because it curled so tightly at the back. They teased Richard about his, too.'

Roger was smiling as he said: 'The observant eye of the artist, you see.'

'Detective.'

'I feel such a *pig*!' said Janet in a subdued voice.

'Pour me out some more coffee and all will be forgiven.' Roger smiled at her. '*And* don't tell me I'm not playing fair if I go and see Coppell.'

'You'd certainly better go and see him,' Janet said. 'If he comes here I might fly at him.' She looked at the photograph and then at Roger, bewilderment in her eyes. 'All the same, it really does look like you. That scar makes it almost incredible that it isn't.'

'It's not such a coincidence as all that,' remarked Martin. 'Look how many people have broken noses or snaggle teeth or quick tempers—' He was grinning broadly at his mother.

'I don't really think you've improved,' Janet said. 'Darling, why don't we go upstairs and talk while your father telephones Coppell. We've so much to tell each other—' She broke off, drew in a deep breath, and gasped: 'Heavens, I haven't told you about *Anne*! She must be wondering what on earth's been going on. Anne—' she began, and told Martin much that he already knew as they went upstairs.

Roger watched them go.

When they were talking to Anne Claire, he went into the kitchen and rinsed his hands and face in cold water from the tap, dried thoroughly and thoughtfully, then went along to the front room, carrying the two photographs. By the side of a large armchair, which had become so shaped to his body that it was the acme of comfort, was a telephone on a small table, with a list of private numbers of senior officers at the Yard by its side. He did not open it for Coppell's number at first, however, but leaned back and closed his eyes. He was tired, but that wasn't the reason for his relaxing. He wanted to think; be sure he had all the facts clear in his mind so that he could talk with complete knowledge to Coppell; but there was more. He wanted to see the implications of this, if there were any; wanted to know what conclusions could be drawn, whether the likeness was sheer coincidence or whether there was some other possible significance. At last, he glanced at his watch. It was half-past eleven, and if Coppell had gone to bed he wouldn't be in his best mood – and he wasn't prone to good moods anyway.

But he had been here; broken in, or—

Roger smiled very faintly to himself and then looked up the number. Coppell lived in Camberwell; somehow the south of the river suited him. The dialling sound began; six *brrr-brrrs* and he was either asleep or out.

At last, the ringing sound broke, and Coppell growled: 'Commander Coppell speaking.'

'Good evening, sir,' said Roger, his voice non-committal, 'this is West. Would you mind answering me a simple question?'

Coppell's normal reaction would be something to the effect that *he* was the one to ask the questions. Instead, in a much quieter voice than usual, he said:

'Depends what it is.'

'How did you get into my house tonight?'

'I had a key,' Coppell said. 'From way back.'

'Did you apply for a search warrant?'

'No.' Coppell spoke bluntly. 'News of search warrants gets out. Thought I'd better handle this one myself.'

'Thank you, sir,' Roger said. 'So no one else knows of this – ah – suspicion?'

'Five senior officers know about the photograph and reported the likeness and the scar under your chin to me. No reason to believe they'll talk, unless someone gives them cause. You, say, or me.'

'I hope neither of us need to,' Roger said. 'The photograph isn't of me, sir.'

'Can you prove it?'

'I've satisfied my wife without trouble.'

Coppell gave a half-laugh. 'Have you satisfied that son of yours?'

'Yes, sir.'

'He's quite a man,' Coppell said, 'he could have broken my arm and he did knock me out with a punch the like of which I haven't felt for many a long day. I used to box, you know.'

'He'll be glad to talk to you about it, sir,' said Roger. 'Would you like to see me at once?'

After a pause Coppell asked: 'Why?'

'There are one or two angles we might be able to think about before morning,' Roger told him.

Coppell hesitated again, and then he asked: 'Won't the telephone do?'

'If that's what you prefer, sir.'

'It is.'

'Very well,' Roger said. With half of his mind he wondered why Coppell was so positive. Was his wife away? Was he – well, none of his, Roger's, business.

Was it just that he did not want to wait the twenty minutes or so it would take Roger to get to Camberwell, or the fuss of making coffee or serving drinks? Oh, nonsense! 'I think the evidence – condition, length and texture of hair – is quite conclusive but we'll need our photographic lab boys on it first thing in the morning. The second thing is – that scar.'

'Damned peculiar,' Coppell said.

'Yes. I can understand a man having a scar the same shape, and in the same place, as mine, but I can't understand him looking so much like me.'

He left the words hanging – and they hung for a long time before Coppell roared in his best manner:

'What the devil are you driving at, West?'

'I thought it was obvious, sir.'

'Well, it isn't obvious to me – let's have it, and no fancy words.'

'The man apparently looks very like me. He has a scar on the underside of his chin, and allows himself to be photographed so that the scar shows. He then murders the woman police officer but not until she's sent out the photograph. And but for one thing I would say it looks as if he wants it to be thought that he is me.'

Coppell did him the compliment of breathing hard into the telephone but not saying a word.

'And I think we ought to make finding out the reason absolute priority.'

Coppell was still breathing hard, but this time he did ask a question.

'You said "but for one thing". What thing?'

'Police Officer Brace didn't say who it was.'

'There's an answer to that,' said Coppell.

'I'll be glad to hear it, sir.'

'Suppose she sent an earlier message saying it was

you, but the message didn't reach us. That way she wouldn't think it necessary to repeat the identification. In any case the photograph would surely be enough. Wouldn't it? Eh?'

'Probably,' Roger agreed, and then because there was no point in leaving anything in the air, he went on: 'I'm sure you're right, sir. Where is the body now?'

'The mortuary in Kingham Street.'

'Who did the autopsy, sir?'

'Your pal Appleby,' answered Coppell.

'Good,' Roger said. 'I'd like to go and see him in the morning before coming into the office. Who's in charge of my investigation?'

Coppell growled: 'Superintendent Trannion.'

'It's a long time since I worked with St. Matt,' said Roger, and then caught himself out in a yawn. 'Well, that's all from my end, sir. If you'd like a recap—'

'I don't need a recap,' Coppell interrupted. 'You think this may be a deliberate frame to make this bandit look like you, and you think we should give priority to finding out why?'

'Precisely, sir.'

'I'll discuss it with the Commissioner in the morning,' Coppell said. 'He is keeping a personal eye on this case.' He rang off, without a 'goodbye' and without a word of explanation, obviously having held the last announcement in reserve so that he could have the last word.

Slowly, Roger replaced the receiver.

'If Jacob Trevillion's got a hand in this, he's worried,' he said aloud. And after a pause, he went on: 'Well it won't do him any harm to be worried for a while.' He leaned back in the chair, head resting comfortably and back well-supported. He could sleep here almost as well as he could in bed. He allowed his thoughts to drift for a few more minutes and then stood up, yawned hugely, closed the confidential telephone book and put it away, then went into the hall. He could hear voices from upstairs, none from downstairs. He went to the kitchen, where a note was propped up against the coffee pot:

I've gone up, darling. Don't forget to put out the lights. Then, in blacker, underlined letters: *Sorry, truly sorry.* He put out the lights and went towards the sounds of voices only to stop abruptly; only Martin's and the girl Anne's sounded, Martin talking earnestly, the girl doing most of the listening.

'Well, I suppose it's an attitude of mind, really, it has nothing to do with where you are. . . I liked Australia although it's a bit hot in the summer, but. . . well, I couldn't see myself marrying an Australian girl. There's a difference in attitudes and in thinking. I – oh, I don't know. Talking a lot of jim-jam really, I suppose.'

'Nonsense! It's been fascinating,' Anne Claire said.

'You should hear my brother, he really *is* fascinating,' said Martin. 'Well, time to turn in, I suppose. I'm jolly glad you're here, I must say!'

'And I couldn't be more glad that you are,' Anne answered.

Roger slipped into the bedroom, moving so that Martin wouldn't see him as he came out of the girl's room. Next moment he nearly jumped out of his skin, for there was Janet surreptitiously moving away from the door. She gave him a welcoming smile, but there was something in the expression of her eyes which told him that her attention wasn't wholly focussed on him.

'Did you hear them?' she asked.

'Who?'

'Don't be dense. Martin and Anne.'

'They were saying goodnight—'

'Saying goodnight! Is *that* all you see in it?' exclaimed Janet. 'I've never *seen* a clearer case of love at first sight on both sides. I know Martin's impressionable, bless him, but Anne—'

'You are an incurable romantic,' Roger said firmly. 'Get into bed, my love, this may be our last chance for a frolic for a long time, I have a big assignment coming my way.'

Janet said dreamily: 'I liked her from the moment I first saw her. Wouldn't it be wonderful. . .'

8

Evidence or Proof?

ROGER WOKE SOON after seven o'clock next morning with a heavy pressure at the back of his head. This was going to be a day with a dull headache, and he couldn't think why; he and Janet had shared only one bottle of Niersteiner the previous night. Then he remembered: the shock of finding Martin home, the shock and tension of Janet's attitude, the talk with Coppell. 'Cold shower, quick,' he told himself and got out of bed cautiously, for Janet was fast asleep, only the top of her dark head was showing. He went out onto the landing and heard the latch of the bathroom door go. Damn! That was Anne, who was an early riser. Or could it be Martin? Disgruntled on the one hand, elated because of Martin's homecoming, worried by the peculiar job which was being thrust upon him, he went downstairs and made himself tea, keeping an ear cocked for sounds from the bathroom. He was halfway through his first cup when light footsteps moved across the landing and down the stairs.

Anne appeared at the kitchen door. She gave him a bright 'Good morning!' adding penitently: 'I'm so sorry,'I didn't *mean* to hog the bathroom.'

'Come and have a cup of tea,' Roger suggested, 'five minutes won't make much difference.' He poured out, remembering that she liked a little milk but no sugar. She took the cup from him, then drank with slow enjoyment. 'Ah, the first cup. Nothing like it.' She had washed off her night creams or whatever she used but put on no make-up. Her hair was looser – fluffier – than usual, softening her features. She wore a strawberry pink dressing-gown of some velvety material which made her look more feminine than usual.

'Penny for them,' she said.

'I was wondering what you think of Martin,' he countered.

'The right thing would be to pretend I believe you, but I don't really think I do.' Mischief glowed in her eyes.

Roger's expression was as amused as her own.

'Then what do you think I was thinking about?' he asked.

'Me,' she answered promptly, and when he neither agreed nor denied it, she went on coaxingly: 'Come on, own up. Martin has told me how honest you are, he spent at least half-an-hour last night telling me! You can't be honest with him and dishonest with me, now can you?'

'No,' Roger said, 'that's true enough. And I can't get to the office by nine o'clock if I don't shower and shave and have my breakfast.' He downed the last of the tea, then jumped to his feet. He had almost reached the door when he paused, and looked back. 'The truth, the whole truth and nothing but the truth is asking rather a lot of any man, but I'll have a shot at it. I was thinking that you are a very nice young woman, and I like you a lot. I was thinking that if ever I have a daughter-in-law I hope she'll be like you – unless you're very different from the person you've been showing me these last few weeks. Can you cook bacon and eggs?'

'You know very well that I can!'

'Half-an-hour?' suggested Roger. 'That would be just right.' He gave her a broad grin and then hurried upstairs.

Half-an-hour later almost to the minute he went back into the kitchen, to find her in a flowered smock, bending solicitously over the toaster. Over breakfast they talked of trivialities, lightly and inconsequently. Nothing deeper was mentioned, but Roger decided that he had meant what he said in their earlier conversation.

Janet was still asleep; Martin still locked in his room. Anne, who worked in a picture-framing and bric-à-brac shop in Chelsea, would have to leave soon after he did.

'Sure I can't give you a lift?' he asked.

She shook her head, her good-humoured camaraderie suddenly leaving her, anxiety taking its place.

'I haven't offended you, have I?'

He looked at her very steadily, and said: 'You're one of the brightest things in my life. You belong somehow – as much as Martin, as much as Richard.'

'Oh, bless you!' she exclaimed. 'Bless you!'

He thought there were tears in her eyes when he left the house, and went to the garage. He was at the kerb, restarting the engine, when Janet appeared at an upstairs window, waving. He blew her a kiss as he drove off; he wasn't really thinking about her but of what he had just said to Anne Claire. The question of importance was: had he meant it?

Aloud, he said: 'I meant it all right.'

Then he turned into King's Road and began to concentrate on his driving.

*   *   *

There were the two worlds.

There was the world at home, usually relaxed, sometimes emotionally explosive, familiar, as full of the past as of the present – perhaps more full of the past. And there was the world of the police, utterly different if just as familiar; a frightening world if one thought or worried about it too much; and in his way, he was a worrier. He did not like the new building with its main entrance in Broadway and a side entrance in Queen Victoria Street, which the C.I.D. men usually preferred. He took the main entrance where there would be many more people and he would soon know if there were any rumours on the wing about him. One developed a kind of sixth sense about such things.

This morning there was none: only the usual good-mornings. 'Hi, Handsome!' 'Sleep late, Handsome?' 'Good morning, good morning, good morning.' He went up in the lift to the fourth floor, the main floor for C.I.D. men. His own office was along on the right, large, square, with contemporary furniture; cold-looking. Leading off this was a smaller room where his regular *aide,* Detective Sergeant Hadley worked: or more correctly both slaved and unequivocally admired. It was an admiration that could be irritating, for it embraced both the good and the not-so-good equally.

Roger poked his head round the communicating door – and looked into an empty office. He let the door close and turned to his desk finding some piles of paper and a note: *Been sent out on a special job, sir – be back by eleven a.m.*

Well, that was that. Roger looked out onto an array of houses and side streets and wished they were the Thames and the Embankment. Well, they weren't. He took out some notes he had made last night and the first was: *Call Appleby.* Dan Appleby was the best-known and in his, Roger's, opinion the best pathologist at the Home Office. He worked almost exclusively for the Yard, and a number of unusual cases on which they had worked together had made them good friends. He put in a call, knowing that if Appleby was actually performing an operation he would not come to the telephone. But soon he was on the line, speaking with his rather high-pitched voice and his stammer, which falsely suggested he was diffident or nervous.

'D-D-D-Dan Appleby h-h-here.'

'Dan,' Roger said. 'This is—'

'I thought I'd s-s-soon be hearing from y-y-you,' Appleby stated, 'and the b-b-best thing is for me to c-c-come and see you or y-y-you to come and see m-m-me. We might even have lun-lun-lunch together!' he exclaimed, as if taken by sudden inspiration.

'I wish I could,' Roger said, 'but I doubt if I'll have time to snatch more than a sandwich. And I need some information from you quickly. Five minutes on the telephone—'

'T-t-tell you what,' interrupted Appleby. 'We'll have coffee. You can't pretend you haven't t-t-time for that. The R.A.C. at eleven o'clock. S-s-splendid, old chap!' And he rang off.

Appleby was not only the best Home Office pathologist in the business, he was one of the shrewdest men of Roger's acquaintance. He wanted to talk where they couldn't be observed, and if that was what he wanted then it was necessary. Roger put the receiver down and pushed the telephone aside. Coppell might send for him at any time, and if the Commissioner were involved it might be impossible to leave the office in time to reach the Royal Automobile Club. There was one way to find out, and he dialled Coppell on the inter-phone.

'Oh, I wondered when I would be hearing from you,' Coppell said, with a note of complaint in his voice. 'Have you got that other photograph with you?'

'One is on the way from the *Graphic*,' Roger answered; and marvelled that he could have forgotten so obvious a thing as that.

'Well, have some copies made – say eight. We'll match up eight of those and eight of yours – I mean the one that looks like you. Take 'em along to Trannion, and he'll check them out. All clear?'

Roger's heart was beating fast.

'Tried and found guilty, is that it?'

'Don't be a bloody fool. And don't be so jumpy, either, or I'll recommend you for a good long rest. Can't have you working on this case until we know it wasn't you lying on that bed, and you know it.' He paused long enough for that to sink in, and then added gruffly: 'And be ready for an interview with the Commissioner and a few others at two o'clock. Understood?'

'Understood,' Roger said mechanically, and thought: trial.

He was being over-sensitive, of course, and Coppell was unarguably right. Yet the way this was being handled rankled, and might continue to do so for some time. That was bad, because if his mind was preoccupied with emotions he couldn't use it effectively. He pulled a file towards him – and the internal telephone bell rang.

He took off the receiver. 'West.'

'Tidy up every job you're handling, if you're wanted on this one, you won't have time for others until it's over. Oh, and another thing: I had to use your man Hadley for some back work on the bullion job, he's up in Staffordshire now, won't be back for a couple of days.'

Coppell rang off.

It was as well he did; Roger was already forming an angry: 'So as to make sure I'm absolutely on my own.' He sat, fuming; no telephone bell interrupted and no one came in. He *needed* Hadley. There wasn't a better young officer at the Yard and for the last few years Roger and he had built up a *rapport* rare between senior and junior officers. He not only anticipated what Roger would need next, but often made suggestions in an apologetic, even a diffident way as to the best thing to try. It had developed from a relationship in which Roger had doubted if he could ever work with the youth to one in which he often wondered how he would get on without him.

Well, he was going to find out.

The first move in the game was obvious; they were going to indict him. As for the 'few others' with the Commissioner, who were they going to be? Trannion, the smug old hypocrite, or—

'Now stop it!' Roger said aloud. Trannion was certainly smug and seemed pious, but hypocrite – no. He turned up the number of the *Graphic,* whose news editor he knew reasonably well; and the man was in. He listened, and responded promptly:

'I remember the picture. Our chap took it as you were looking upwards – about a week ago. Right?'

'Right.'

'I'll send some prints over. If I haven't enough I'll make some.' He rang off without another word, while Roger opened his briefcase and took out the photograph of the man who wasn't him. He had no doubts at all, and so he had to ask the questions he had asked Coppell the previous night. Who would want to be taken for him, and why?

Of course he couldn't be absolutely sure it wasn't coincidence.

'Coincidence my foot!' he exclaimed, and began to turn over the other case files. None was of any importance, the work had been surprisingly light for some weeks, the lightest period he had known for years. He—

My God!

He pulled the inter-office telephone towards him, and dialled one of his oldest friends at the Yard, then Detective Sergeant now Chief Inspector Bill Sloan; Sloan answered on the instant, and and Roger said: 'Bill, how busy are you?'

'Busy?' groaned Sloan. 'I never seem to stop.'

'Then you're not the man I'm looking for,' Roger said. 'Hope things ease up soon.' He finished going through the files, and decided that any intelligent sergeant could handle them, while Hadley could finish the lot off in a couple of days. He had known that, after a particularly heavy period which even Coppell had realised could lead to a serious breach in his marriage, he needed a holiday. But he hadn't realised how light the load was at the moment. He went down to *Information*. Ten o'clock in the morning was not the busiest time, but a dozen uniformed men were sitting in front of teletype machines at the great conveyor which took all the calls from outside along to a sorting desk for appropriate action. Marriott, a youthful Chief Inspector, was in charge; a man only just tall enough to squeeze into the regulation five foot eight, slightly built and rather delicate looking, yet he could fling a six feet, twenty stone man over his shoulder.

'Good morning, sir!'

'Good morning,' Roger returned. 'Business not too brisk?'

'Welcome change,' said Marriott. 'Sometimes I think this is the nearest thing to hell in London.'

'Like that, is it?' Roger's heart contracted. 'Need more men, as usual?'

'They built this place eight years ago and now it's about big enough for two thirds of our needs. Trouble is—' Mariott stopped, as if suddenly realising that he was talking to a superior and presumably what he was saying was none of his business.

'Go on,' Roger said.

'Well, none of my business I suppose, sir,' said Marriott, 'but the trouble isn't that we're too small and that the whole Force is under strength. The trouble is that there's a damn sight too much crime. It's been increasing slowly for years. One accepts it without much thought, although I'll admit it's worried me sometimes. But now – care to see my chart, sir? I keep one in case there's a call for it. Can't say there often is.'

'Yours not to reason why, yours to make the

information fly,' misquoted Roger, and actually caused Marriott to laugh.

'That's about the size of it, sir,' he said, taking a large folder out of his desk. He opened it, displaying a simple graph, with a rising line in red. He traced it along with one finger. Even before he spoke Roger saw that this line represented the crime rate per thousand head of population in the Metropolitan Police area – and the rise in the past six months had been phenomenal. In some weeks the line of the progress indicator went almost straight up; every week, it climbed steeply.

Marriott pulled this sheet aside and showed another which at first sight was like the chart of falling meteorites; streaks of different-coloured lights, all but two going upwards.

'Here I've coloured a chart for types of crime,' Marriott went on. 'The red line is crimes of violence for gain, the red one with white dashes, violence for no known motive, blue for hold-ups, green for day-time break-ins, black for night—' He broke off and gave a quick, almost sheepish smile. 'The Map Room is much more comprehensive, of course, these just give the picture at a glance, so to speak.'

'They certainly do that,' Roger said thoughtfully. 'What's the one still in the drawer?'

'Oh – er – those.' Marriott actually coloured. 'Well I don't know whether they're relevant, sir, but they show the same as the coloured chart, only division by division. I – er – it worries me a bit, makes me wonder—'

He broke off again, and now his face was almost puce in colour.

'Here they are, sir.'

9

Steps

ROGER STUDIED THE charts with quickening interest. Piccadilly Circus, the Strand, Leicester Square and Notting Hill Gate – in these places one would expect to see a high rate of such crimes as pocket-picking, bag-snatching and shop-lifting, but even so, the figures were surprisingly high.

So were crimes of violence both for profit and without known motive.

Roger handed them back.

'Thanks. What do you gather from them?'

Almost desperately Marriott said: 'It really *isn't* any of my business, sir.'

'Unofficially – all of this is off the record,' Roger went on, 'unless I come and see you about releasing the graphs yourself.'

'You're very good, sir,' Marriott said. 'Well – it does rather look as if the discipline – the thoroughness of precautions – is rather slack, doesn't it?'

'Yes,' Roger answered. 'Too slack.'

'But you do see that if I were to make such a suggestion—'

'I see that if you were asked to make a report based on information which comes through this room you would have to use your graphs, and anyone who studied them would draw obvious conclusions,' Roger said quietly. 'And it could come to that.'

'Meanwhile I'll just keep these by me,' Marriott said.

Roger half-turned, saying: 'Do that,' and then turned to face the other man, suddenly frowning. Marriott looked first puzzled and then alarmed. Roger moved back to his desk and sat on the corner.

'Do you have a camera?' he asked.

'No, sir – why?'

'I'd like to have those graphs photographed in colour,' Roger said. 'I lost the only copy of a piece of evidence that I had, once. Any objection?' When Marriott didn't answer Roger went on: 'One of my sons has a polaroid which takes colour prints without the usual negative. If we take two sets, I can lodge one in my bank and yours wherever you like.' He paused before asking again: 'Any objection?'

'The more I think about it the more I think it's a good idea,' Marriott said. 'Would you take the photographs yourself?'

'Either myself, or my son.'

'Morning or early afternoon is the best time,' Marriott told him, and now there was eagerness in his eyes. 'And the sooner the better, I should think.'

'You couldn't be more right,' agreed Roger, 'I'd like to call my home.' In a few moments he was talking first to Janet, and then to Martin, who sounded in high fettle.

'Why, yes,' he said. 'I can use it. . . Not sure how much film there is and I may not have enough ready cash. . . Okay, I'll ask Mum. . . Royal Automobile Club at half-past eleven, fine. Okay, Pop! See you, I – *hold on*.' He shouted the last two words and Roger held on for a few moments, his ear ringing. Then Janet came on the line.

'Darling,' she said in a subdued voice.

'Hallo,' Roger said, conscious of half-a-dozen pairs of eyes on him.

'I couldn't be more sorry about last night.'

Momentarily, Roger wondered what she was talking about, then quite suddenly he realised, and laughed on a light note, wholly reassuring.

'Forget it. It would have fooled anybody.'

'Well, yes, perhaps. But I'm not "anybody", and it shouldn't have fooled me. I love you, Roger. I love you so very much.'

On the last word, she rang off.

He replaced the receiver slowly, as sure as he could be that she felt what she said with all the emotion in her: and yet if something happened to spark the flame of jealousy again she would behave in exactly the same manner. He gave a sigh of good-tempered exasperation. It was then half-past ten, and he wanted to walk to the R.A.C. which should take no more than twenty minutes. Walking cleared his mind for thinking. He left a note with Marriott where he was going, then went out by the Queen Victoria Street entrance. The sky had cleared and there was a bright sun, but it was still cold.

There were several ways to go to the Royal Automobile Club in Pall Mall; he chose the one which wound through side streets and mews until at last he came within sight of the tops of the trees of St. James's Park; now all he had to do was cross the park and go up the steps into Carlton House Terrace, splendid in its recent reconstruction. He stood there, with the whole panorama of the park stretched before him; the lake, the trees, the flowering shrubs, the huge beds of flowers he couldn't place from here. He sniffed the scent of newly-cut grass – yes, here, actually in the heart of London, and in the distance was the clatter of the big motor mower which was trimming the turf.

Suddenly, he ducked down.

On that instant, something smacked into the stone wall of the steps, and chippings flew about his legs and ankles. Before he could look round, before he even realised what was happening, another smack came close to his face and chippings stung his cheeks and lodged in his hair.

He was instantly, dreadfully, afraid.

If there was someone there deliberately shooting at him, determined to get him, he wouldn't have a chance.

He felt a red-hot pain in his left forearm.

There was a protective iron rail on one side of the steps and he grabbed this with both hands, gritting his teeth against the pain as he hauled himself up until, with a great effort, he could swing himself over. He fell headlong onto the newly turned soil of a flowerbed, had a picture of an elderly woman with a fork in her hands. He rolled over, soil getting into his eyes and mouth and nostrils, almost choking him. When he lay still he was on his back and the woman was closer; she had rammed the fork into the earth, no long holding it as if it were a weapon of defence. He looked about him, and then managed to ask through the soil in his mouth:

'Someone's shooting. Be careful.'

'You come with me, young man,' the woman said, with the calm practicality of one who has lived through two world wars, 'and get that dirt off you.' She helped him with welcome strength and skill until he was on his feet. At the top of the steps was a cloakroom, and she left him there while he took off his jacket and brushed himself down. He looked searchingly through the window, but all he could see were a few people walking along Birdcage Walk and a solitary rider cantering out of sight.

The left sleeve of his shirt was thick with blood.

He rolled this up, gingerly held the wound under the cold tap, saw that it was only a shallow groove which needed attention but wasn't going to get in his way very much. First rinsing out his mouth, then dousing himself under a stream of water which now ran warm, he felt much better. As he finished, the woman came back.

She said severely: 'May I ask, young man, if you are on the run from the police?'

'No,' Roger answered. 'I am—'

Then she saw the wound, blood still welling up but not running so freely.

'Well,' she remarked, 'at least I know that I am not the victim of a practical joke. Have you washed that well?'

'Yes, ma'am.'

'What caused it?'

'A bullet.'

'Oh, dear me. Well hold it under the cold tap again for a moment, while I get the first-aid box. I always keep that at the foot of the main stairs, so handy for gardening accidents. Nurturing flowers appears such a gentle pastime to those who have never done it. Is that hurting?'

'Not much.'

'False courage, young man, is another guise for vanity.' She talked all the time until she was back with a big metal box on which was a faded red cross. 'Now let me see that wound... Have no fear, during both world wars I was a fully trained nursing auxiliary... I shall first bathe it with an antiseptic lotion—' Bottle and cotton wool were both most professionally handled, as she sponged the wound with a strong smelling antiseptic. Next, she spread a salve over a piece of lint and said: 'This will prevent it from sticking.' She taped this in position at either end, and asked: 'Have you any preference for adhesive plaster or a bandage?'

'Which do you think is best?' he asked.

'A bandage here – it need not be too big for the sleeve, and it prevents any movement.' Her wrinkled fingers moved deftly. 'Now – you realise that for comfort as well as for quicker healing you will need a sling, don't you?'

Slowly, Roger said: 'I hadn't. But I'll take your word for it.'

'You are an understanding young man,' she approved, 'but then, you have been frightened. Are you aware that it is really my duty to report this whole incident to the police?'

Roger smiled.

'Yes.'

'I hope you will come upstairs and have some coffee with plenty of sugar in it while we discuss—'

'I really must go, I'm afraid,' Roger said. 'If you could ring for a taxi I would be more than grateful.' He took out his card and showed it to her. She read it, with a sniff of amusement.

'Good gracious, and here am I advising you to tell the police. But Superintendent, you really need rest, and coffee—'

'I've an appointment I mustn't break,' Roger said, 'but there's one thing I would dearly love.'

'What is that, Superintendent?'

'To come and have coffee – or tea if that would be better – just as soon as this case is over.'

'Why, that would be delightful!' she declared. 'And I shall hold you to it, have no doubt. As for a taxi, they are very difficult at this time of morning, my husband will be happy to take you wherever you wish to go.'

Her husband, small wrinkled, gnome-like, appeared almost more imperturbable than she. He seemed happy enough to leave his *Times* crossword puzzle and his high-backed winged chair in a book-lined study to take Roger to the club.

'Most interesting place, did you know? I knew it before the war when it was the German Embassy. Actually met Kaiser Wilhelm there myself – I was a junior in the Diplomatic Corps in those days. Such a pity, such a pity. If there'd been no first world war, there would have been no second world war. No Kaiser Wilhelm being pushed by his politicians and so no Hitler. Strange, eerie life, Mr. – ah – Superintendent West. Did you ever pause to reflect. . .' He talked as he drove with an assured skill at least as great as his wife's at first-aid, threading serenely through the traffic in his ancient Rolls-Royce. 'Eerie, is perhaps the word. I mean, the point is, if you hadn't walked down those steps as that lunatic shot at you, and if my wife hadn't been working in the garden – mind you, she usually is – and I hadn't stayed in this morning, whatever happens after your forthcoming meeting at the R.A.C. might have been quite different.'

'Yes, indeed,' Roger agreed, happy not to talk. His arm was throbbing badly.

They turned at last. Pall Mall, from the Trafalgar Square end. The driver began to slow down.

'Mr. West,' he said, 'I wonder if you could help me. I've a problem that has been worrying me most of the morning. A second opinion, unhampered by overlong brooding, is so often successful. Number 17, across. The clue is 'Instrument is harp, not piano, girl concludes''. Ah, here we are.' A tall, elderly doorman came forward to open the door. 'I should never have worried you. Do look after that arm. And be careful.'

'How about harmonica?' suggested Roger.

'I beg your pardon?'

'Harmonica,' Roger repeated.

'Oh, my dear fellow! Harmonica! Of course. I shall be forever in your debt. Do come and have tea some day. Soon. Goodbye, goodbye. Harmonica, of course!'

It was a quarter-past eleven.

In the main hallway of the Club was a very old car, more brass than steel, with huge, solid-rubber tyres, and standing by the rope which cordoned this off was a tall, thin, rather ungainly man, the same kind of build as Chief Superintendent Partridge. He was reading the details of the veteran car and over his shoulder Roger read: *Darracq, 1893*. The man half-turned as Roger said:

'I'm sorry I'm late.'

Dan Appleby looked at the sling and asked: 'Been in the wars before or after our appointment?'

'After.'

'Roger,' stated Appleby, 'you see in f-f-front of you a very f-f-frightened man.' Roger had never heard him say anything remotely like that, yet looking into

Appleby's rather pale blue-grey eyes he had a sense that the remark was meant to be taken seriously. 'Come and find a quiet corner.' He led the way into the huge smoking-room with its dark murals and darker leather chairs, so placed that two people could talk with little risk of being overheard. As he ushered Roger to a spot he had obviously pre-selected, a maid appeared at his shoulder.

'Would you like your coffee now, sir?'

'Please,' said Appleby, and waited for Roger to sit down. Then without preamble or the slightest hesitation and in a voice which was much freer from the stammer than usual, he stated: 'Official opinion. No reasonable d-d-doubt. The woman taken out of the Thames and identified as Alice B-B-Brace was wearing her clothes, had the same kind of f-f-figure, same colour hair, almost identical f-f-features, was approximately the same age, b-b-but was/is *not* Alice Brace. I c-c-can understand anyone im-im-impersonating the living, but why sh-sh-should anyone want to impersonate the dead?'

10

Impersonation – Dead or Alive

ROGER HEARD THE words but did not at first take
them in. 'Why should anyone want to impersonate
the dead?' He was aware of Appleby watching him
intently; the pathologist could always be relied on not
to push too hard. The girl coming up with coffee gave
even longer respite, and Appleby poured out, black,
and pushed the hot milk round so that Roger could
pick up the jug. He poured a little, sipped, and then
said:

'If it comes to that, why should they try to impersonate a policeman, alive or dead.' He took out the zip-
fastened briefcase and extracted the two pictures – the
one a clipping of the newspaper, the other the enlargement sent out by Alice Brace.

Appleby considered them, looked up, and asked:

'W-w-what happened to you j-j-just now?'

'I was shot.'

'This case?'

'It wouldn't surprise me.'

'Then we add a new dimension. Why impersonate
you and when on the point of success, try to kill you?'

'Kill?' Roger asked. 'Or frighten?'

'Why frighten?'

'Dan,' Roger said, 'there's to be a kind of trial by my

peers this afternoon, to find out whether I'm being impersonated or playing a double game.'

'B-b-bloody fools!' ejaculated Appleby.

'Thanks. My point is I need someone unprejudiced, to talk to.'

'Such as me?'

'Yes.'

'Talk on.'

'The first inkling I had of this was last night,' Roger said, sipping coffee and explaining as much as he needed to about Martin. 'One or two things I've now discovered is that my work of late has been very light, whereas the Yard's been up to its neck in urgent jobs.' When Appleby didn't answer, he went on: 'Some of the urgent jobs should have come to me.'

'So – have they suspected you for some time, and have they been watching you. Have you any idea?'

'Not the foggiest,' Roger said. 'There's talk of a meeting with my peers and I think they've met before on this job, leaving me out.'

'Can't spare you?' hazarded Appleby.

'They'd work me to death normally,' Roger answered. 'I am ordered to clear all my other cases off my desk.'

'Ready to be fired or ready to be assigned to a different job?'

Roger shrugged.

'Any real idea which?' Appleby persisted.

'No,' answered Roger with complete candour, 'in some ways I am so angry about it I could just blow up.'

'Don't blow up,' pleaded Appleby. 'This Policewoman Brace – did you know her?'

'Slightly.'

'I offer myself as a living sacrifice,' Appleby said. 'Ever anything between you?'

'No. I doubt if I've often been near enough to her to hold hands. Besides—'

'I know, I know, faithful unto death. Are you feeling all right?'

'Not at my best,' Roger confessed. 'My arm's hurting like blazes and I didn't exactly hit the ground like a feather-weight. I ache.'

'My remedy for all ills,' advised Appleby, fishing in his jacket pocket. He brought out a small white box. 'Two, every four hours, and if you are used to taking them, three or four every four hours.' He unfastened the box which had a special kind of catch, and added: 'A friend sent them. They're called pill toters.' He shook three out close to Roger's cup, and then snapped the lid back and went on briskly: 'I knew you must be feeling as if you'd been dragged through a hedge backwards.'

'Why?'

'You haven't asked me how come I'm so sure about Alice Brace.'

Roger, picking up the pills, actually knocked one onto the floor, and let it lie as he asked:

'How are you so sure she isn't Alice Brace?'

'Because Alice Brace had an operation for an appendix, three years ago, and—'

'It's in her police record, and this woman hasn't got a scar!'

'Such brilliance,' said Appleby, picking up the pill, dropping it into an ashtray and taking another from his pill toter. 'I know we are all said to eat a peck of dirt before we die, but I think we should take it inadvertently. Take 'em.' Roger took all three tablets and washed them down with coffee, his heart still hammering under the discovery. 'I can give you a picture of the dead woman's tummy, unscarred, or a whole full length, also unscarred, as evidence,' he offered.

'Both please,' Roger said.

'Ghoul.'

'Trannion is in charge of the Committee of Inquiry.'

'Oh, is he,' Appleby opened a square black attaché case and took out two photographs and a copy of a sheet marked: *Alice Brace, Medical History.*

'Thanks,' said Roger warmly.

'My pleasure. Any other immediate questions, Handsome?'

Roger didn't answer for what seemed a long time, but Appleby didn't interrupt, simply studied the cutting from the *Globe* and the print this woman had sent to the Yard. Then he poured himself out more coffee, draining the pot, and asked: 'How many?'

Appleby considered the question and countered with another.

'How many other impersonations?'

'Yes.'

'Where?'

Roger in turn considered the question and in turn countered with another.

'In the Force or outside?'

'Yes.'

'Hell of a question.'

'Got to be asked, got to be answered,' replied Appleby. 'Can you take advice or should it wait for a brighter day?'

'In view of my arm, you're safe enough.'

'I should have thought of that,' Appleby said.

'Perhaps we should both resign and go into partnership for finding lost cats or erring spouses.' He leaned forward, looking very serious, even worried, and went on: 'Don't ask the question of anyone except the very top dogs,' he urged. 'Don't share it with Brother Trannion or anyone else. Let the idea play around in your mind for a while before you let it out on anyone. Because, oh Roger boy, this could be dynamite. How many? Two we know of, ten, twenty, thirty—' He broke off.

'I think we'll stop at two,' Roger said. 'For now. Dan, I must be going. This has been a most stimulating half-hour.'

'For me, too. How is Martin?'

'He seems fine, but I haven't been able to talk to him long enough to find out why he's come back,' Roger answered. 'He's always been unpredictable; reaches a stage where he can't stand the situation he's in any longer, and simply walks out.'

'That's all right, while he's single,' observed Appleby. 'I'd like to meet him.'

'Come over to dinner one night soon,' said Roger. 'I'll have Janet call you.'

'I'd love that,' Appleby said soberly. They were walking slowly towards the main smoking-room door, now; only a dozen people were in earshot and they seemed immersed in their newspapers.

'Good. How—' Roger hesitated. 'How are you finding things?'

'In my new bachelorhood? Oh, not so bad,' Appleby replied, with a wry smile suggesting that things were not so good in fact. 'Don't get me wrong, Roger – I am still devoutly glad that the marriage is ended and it didn't even sting when I heard she was marrying again. Felt a pang for the other chap, but who knows, I may have driven her to drink. But – well, it's lonely. I think a man has to learn to live on his own.'

'No one else who interests you?'

'No!' answered Appleby. 'Not remotely. Still, it's early days yet. How's young Hadley getting on?'

'First-class,' Roger said, and did not say that Hadley had been sent up to the Midlands out of the way. As they walked together past the venerable Darracq and down the carpeted stairs, one of the porters, elderly, grey-haired, very erect in bearing, came forward.

'Excuse me, Superintendent,' he said. 'It *is* Superintendent West, isn't it?'

'Yes. Who – good lord! Tom Scottsdale!' Roger felt a sudden warmth of feeling for an ex-Yard man whom he hadn't seen for years. Many of them, whose pensions were not too generous, supplemented them with such jobs as these, or with private security firms. 'How long have you been here?'

'Better part of six months, sir and it's not so bad,' Scottsdale answered. 'Er – there's something I ought to say to you in private, sir – I'd have made myself known in any case but there's a special reason.' He glanced apologetically at Appleby, who said: 'Dammit, I forgot to get my *Times*,' and turned and hurried away.

'Well?' asked Roger.

'Sir,' said Scottsdale, 'I can't be positive but I *think* you're being followed.'

Roger's heart missed a beat.

'Go on.'

'I saw you arrive, sir – I was the man who opened your car door – and a taxi stopped not far behind you. . . Didn't pull into the rank, and no one got out. It turned into St. James's Square, but there was something – well, you know how things are, sir, never lose your nose for something a bit peculiar.'

'No,' Roger said.

'Well, I had my break soon afterwards, and walked round the square – often do on a nice day, keeps you in trim, I always say. Well, sir, that taxi is parked only a few cars along across the road, with a passenger in it and the flag down. I just thought you ought to know, sir.'

'You couldn't be more right,' Roger said warmly, 'I'm having some bother at the moment. Is there any way of identifying the car?'

'Just it's number plate, sir – YCA 142.'

'Number plates can be changed. No dents, scars, broken windows, anything like that?'

Scottsdale considered.

'Well, sir – it's got a label, a transfer of some kind, on the windscreen which someone's tried to pull off without much luck. On the left-hand side, top.'

'Good!' Roger's eyes were glowing, and he gripped the other's forearm. 'Now I want to go and call the Yard.' He hurried up to the phone booth, beckoning Appleby who had a newspaper in his right hand and was looking rather forlorn. Roger dialled 999 and said: 'Police, please.' Almost immediately he was answered by one of the men sitting at the big conveyor in the *Information* Room. 'Is Mr Marriott there?. . . This is Superintendent West.' Again he had only the briefest of waits before Marriott came on the line.

'Yes, sir?'

'I think I'm being followed by a man in a taxi, black, present number YCA 142,' Roger said, with great

deliberation. 'At the moment I'm at the Royal·
Automobile Club, waiting in the hall. I'd like two
vehicles not identifiable as police cars to watch the
taxi – and I'd like one of our taxis, a brown one, to pull
up outside the R.A.C. and drop a passenger and then
pick me up. Is that clear?'

'Yes, sir.'

'Fine,' Roger said. 'I can't be sure, but this man may
have a gun.' He rang off, and looked hard at Appleby,
who had not missed a word and now knew the full
significance oi the ex-policeman's message.

Then, Roger became aware of someone standing
close by him.

He was always sensitive to the unemphasised
presence of another, and this morning he was more
sensitive than ever. He did not want to let the other
know he was aware; after all, it could be someone who
wanted to use the telephone.

The 'someone' moved.

'Gosh, Dad,' Martin said in tones of deep interest,
'things really are hotting up, aren't they? Anything I
can do?'

* * *

Roger found himself chuckling; Martin's eyebrows
rose, but nothing really surprised him about his father.
Appleby, realising at once who the 'stranger' was,
watched the reactions of father and son and thought
how different they were and yet, in some ways, how
alike. There was strength in each mouth and jaw, and
the eyes and forehead were almost identical. For the
occasion Martin had put on a grey tweed suit in which
he looked both young and eager.

'Yes,' Roger said, 'and the first job could be extremely important. Do you remember Dr. Appleby, by the way?'

'The pathologist? I believe we did meet once, sir,' Martin said. 'How are you?'

'Recovering from what I just heard your father say on the telephone,' said Appleby, drily.

'Dad, what *is* going on?'

'I'm in the process of finding out. Dan, could you go with Martin to the Yard and introduce him to Chief Inspector Marriott of *Information* – he'll know you – and tell Mariott we need the photographs of those diagrams more urgently than ever? He'll tell you all about it,' Roger added to Martin. 'I hope you've got plenty of film.'

'Ten poundsworth,' Martin answered, as if that must be enough film for a year. 'But Dad, couldn't I follow you?'

'No,' Roger said, simply, and Martin, knowing his father, made no protest.

He and Appleby left the Club together, Martin picking up a heavy-looking suitcase from the porter's lodge. Roger, waiting, was tempted to go and look for that taxi but resisted the impulse. It seemed only a few minutes before a cab in a chocolate brown colour drew up and deposited a passenger, and Roger went out and got in.

'Where to, sir?' the Yard driver asked.

'I think we'll take Lambeth Bridge and then head for Camberwell,' Roger replied. 'We want to lead the chap far enough to be sure our other chaps have picked him up, and won't lose him.'

'Right, sir,' the driver said.

A moment later they passed the end of St. James's

Square, and at that very moment a black taxi with a partly removed sticker on the windscreen pulled into Pall Mall.

Its number had been changed to EBZ 432.

11

Chase and Scramble

ROGER'S DRIVER CROSSED the lines of traffic, making for Clarence House and St. James's Park. The other driver was caught in two swift-moving streams of cars and had to hold back. Roger was tempted to tell his man what to do – turn right towards the Palace where crowds were bound to give them an excuse to be stuck, but this man would be a Flying Squad driver and would know his business inside out.

So Roger said: 'It's just possible they'll try to blow my head off.' His level voice took the melodrama out of the words.

The driver, a phlegmatic-looking man, said equably: 'We can't allow that, sir, can we?'

Roger started a laugh. 'I'd prefer it if we didn't. Do you know what we've got for company?'

'Green van marked *Television, Radio and Recorder Specialists,*' answered the driver, 'and a white one marked *Mardi's Electronic Printers. Bloody fool*!'

'What's he done?'

'Cut across another taxi, sir – I'll say one thing. They don't want to lose you. I'm in radio contact with the other two vehicles, sir. Like to talk to them?'

'Please. Has the taxi caught up?'

'Nearly. I think I'll go up to Horse Guards and then Parliament Square.'

'Up to you,' Roger answered. He unhooked the receiver fastened to the dashboard of the cab, and immediately a man said in broad Cockney:

'Car ZA.'

Another man said in an unmistakable Yorkshire accent: 'Car F – FATHER, E – EDWARD.'

'Can you two hear each other as well as me?' asked Roger.

'Yes, sir,' said the Yorkshire man.

'Roger,' said the Cockney.

'This is Superintendent West—'

'Oh, Gawd,' interrupted the Cockney. 'Trust me to put my plates of meat in it. Won't use "Roger" again, sir.'

'Make it Brown Dog,' Roger said, chuckling. There was something exciting in what was happening; exciting, too, in the knowledge that the police were able to work together so closely, using a wavelength the following cab certainly couldn't pick up. 'What instructions have you had?'

'To follow the brown cab and the black cab, and take one each if they split up.'

'As a basic rule, follow that,' ordered Roger. 'The main job is to find out where the black cab goes, whether it makes any calls or meets other cabs so that the occupants can talk, get descriptions and if possible photographs of drivers, passengers and anyone they talk to. Are you equipped?'

'Aye, sir,' said the Yorkshire man.

'Brown Dog,' answered the Cockney.

'They – I mean the people in the cab or someone

they contact – may make an attack on me. You still follow the cab. That's absolute priority.'

'Yes, sir.'

'And when you've run them to earth try not to let them know it,' said Roger. He rang off before the others could speak again. His own cab was in Parliament Square.

'They're manoeuvring for the middle lane and Victoria Street, sir – assuming you're going to the Yard,' his driver informed him.

'Go along the Embankment,' Roger ordered, 'and across – keep Camberwell as the destination.'

'Very good, sir.'

Roger sat back in the cab, and rested his left arm against his chest. The wound was a nuisance, if the stuff that the little lady had put on didn't begin to give him more comfort soon, he would have to have the dressing changed; she probably still used medicaments which had been popular in the first world war. He smiled slightly to himself.

They were now driving along that stretch of road which ran between Parliament Square and the approach to Lambeth Bridge, a section which was often much emptier than most in London. For a moment he was relaxed; they would soon be over the bridge, and—

'Sir,' the driver said calmly. 'They're closing up on us.'

Roger caught his breath.

'Fast?'

'As fast as the traffic will allow. Shall I go faster?'

'No,' Roger said. 'Just hold that wheel – they're not after you, they're after me.'

'They're coming up on the outside.' There was

nothing remotely phlegmatic about the driver now, anxiety made his voice sharpen; but his hands were loose on the wheel. 'Duck, sir!'

Roger, in the far corner from the overtaking cab, saw its nose, then its windscreen, and knew that it was putting on an exceptional burst of speed. He saw the man sitting by the driver, and the gun in his hand, held close to the body so that it wasn't easy to see. Roger saw a broad face with a broad nose – and then threw himself to the right. He heard the crack of the shot; the glass did not shatter but a hole leapt into it. He heard two more shots; sharp cracks. The black cab passed. A green van and then a white one followed – Cars ZA and FE. His own car came to a surprisingly steady standstill, and the driver was out of his door and looking in at Roger in a trice.

'You all right, sir?'

'Yes,' Roger said, 'but wait a minute.' His mind began to work as fast as it had ever done. 'Call the Yard, have one of our ambulance cars come and get me. It can drop me at St. George's and I can be admitted as seriously hurt.' He gave his broadest grin. 'And if you were to ask me why I couldn't tell you yet.'

The driver drew a deep breath.

'The only thing I care about is that you're all right. They really mean to get you, sir, don't they?' He was already taking the receiver off its hook, while pedestrians were drawing up, intently curious. In the distance a policeman was coming towards them with surprising speed, only his helmet showing above the crowd.

Roger felt as if all the blood had been drained out of his body. Reaction, of course, reaction from some loss of blood, plus the fact that he had twice been within an ace of death.

The driver was talking.

The policeman was saying in an unexpectedly deep voice: 'Move back, please, move *back*.'

Roger opened his eyes – and saw, very close to the open door, close to the driver, a man he had seen from the steps that morning.

And in the man's hand was a small automatic pistol.

*   *   *

Death glared at him.

Death, which he had escaped by inches twice already that day.

He was too shocked to move; mesmerised.

He could not even think the obvious things: that the brown cab had been followed, that those who wished him dead were willing to take fantastic chances; that this man must know that he faced certain capture, he would never escape through the crowd which the policeman was trying to force back.

He *saw* the finger move on the trigger.

He felt as if his whole body, his head, his mind and heart, were splitting asunder.

Yet he did not die, for no bullet struck him, although in those few panic-stricken seconds he did not know why. Knowledge came to him later as he was driven away in an ambulance, the whole scene as vivid as if it were happening again, except for the dreadful explosion in his head and in his body.

*   *   *

The driver of the Yard's taxi had an unremarkable name: Percy Briggs.

He sat at the wheel of his cab, which was lawfully licensed, day in and day out, sometimes actually plying for hire. He was Buddha-like in his solidity and stillness and he moved less of his body than ten average taxi drivers put together.

He had, like many of the men at the Yard who were never likely to rise above the rank of sergeant, certain favourite superiors. He did not hero-worship them, for his was not a romantic mind; but he followed their cases with interest, admired their methods, respected them as men, although he came in contact with very few of them.

In his early days in the Force, out on the beat before the days of walkie-talkies and fast patrol cars, he had had little time for West: too glamorous, too much of a show-off, always around when there was publicity and at the end of a case, but getting his results from the labour of others, had been his summing up.

Then one day, he had been on the fringe of a job West was handling. Up on the roof of a fire-gutted building, a roof which might cave in at any moment, was a man with enough nitro-glycerine in his hand to blow up a whole block of houses. West had sent everyone else out of range and gone up after the man.

Alone.

No one knew how he managed it; everyone knew that he got the nitro away, and then knocked the man out and gave the signal that all was safe and a fire escape should be sent at once.

Briggs didn't exactly hero-worship West as a result; but he put West high above the rest of top policemen.

On this particular day, hearing West give his orders, and then seeing his reaction under fire, Briggs's opinion rose even higher. He wasn't even certain West hadn't been hurt, and hurrying his call for an ambulance, and turning to make sure, he saw what he had never expected to find on the other's face.

Fear.

Terror.

And West was looking at a man who was standing close to the open door of the taxi; a man in whose hand was a gun.

Percy Briggs did not even give himself time to speak or shout, he simply bent his arm and drove his elbow into the man. He heard a gasp, a zutt of sound which he knew came from an automatic air pistol, and he saw West still sitting, as if petrified. *Then* Briggs burst into action. He spun round, grabbed the gunman who was now trying to push into the crowd. He caught him with one great hand by the neck and he shook and shook and shook him again, until people in the crowd called out in protest, and the policeman, now with a second in support, called out sharply:

'Stop that!'

Percy Briggs, the stolid, the phlegmatic, the never-emotional policeman, swung his victim under one arm, bent down and picked up the pistol. This he flourished in the faces of the two policemen.

'This swine just tried to shoot Handsome West. Know who West is? The best bloody copper in London. He's been shot at twice today, and wounded once, and now this little sod tried to shoot him again. *Now* does anyone feel sorry I nearly broke his neck?'

There was a hush, broken only by passing traffic

and the mournful wail of a tug or barge on the Thames. One of the policemen said drily:

'All the same, you'd better let us have him.'

Slowly, Briggs lowered his victim, and almost at the same moment the sound of an ambulance siren came clearly.

*   *   *

Roger was vaguely aware of light and of consciousness. He was aware of an ache in his left arm and also in the side of his head. He was aware that he was somewhere unusual – not the office, not home. He did not feel particularly troubled, even when he began to realise what had happened. This was a hospital, of course, and he was drowsy from some drug. He had a curious feeling that he should be driven by a sense of urgency, but he wasn't.

Next time he opened his eyes he could see more clearly and his head was easier. This was a small, private ward in a hospital; there was a thermometer in a glass by his side, a chart at the foot of his bed, and his arm, much more heavily bandaged than it had been before, lay over the pale green bedspread. It did not ache anything like so much.

It was half-past three.

'That's one conference I didn't get to,' he whispered. 'I wonder if they found me guilty or not guilty.' He actually laughed.

Then he thought of his driver, but for whom he would be dead; he did not even know the man's name. Well, he must find that out.

And he must soon tell someone he was awake and ready to question and be questioned. Had the two Q cars traced the taxi, for instance? Was there any more news of Alice Brace? Why had a woman who looked just like her been murdered? He was beginning to fret and to fidget. He needed to know things, above all *why* was this happening, what was going on?

He stretched out his hand for the telephone by his side, actually dialled the first two digits of the Yard's new number before his hand dropped, and the receiver clattered back into place. His whole body stiff, his head taut, as if his brains were expanding and expanding and trying to find a way out, he lay there. He did not move for perhaps twenty minutes. Only then did he begin to relax, and only after another five minutes did he pick up and draw the telephone towards him and, this time, dial Coppell's direct line. He waited for the ringing sound for so long that he was afraid the man was out, but at last the ringing broke and Coppell rasped:

'Coppell.'

'West here, sir,' Roger said.

'*West*. I thought you were at death's door in hospital.'

'Keep your voice low,' urged Roger. 'I'm on the private line so that I can't be overheard.' Coppell simply grunted, and Roger went on: 'It might be a good idea if officially I do die.'

'What the—' began Coppell, only to add gruffly: 'Go on.'

'Did you know the woman we took out of the river wasn't Detective Officer Brace?'

'You must have had a nasty blow on the head.'

'Check with Appleby,' Roger urged. 'No one's been knocking him about. Someone impersonated her – someone seems to be impersonating me.'

'Give me a minute to think that out,' asked Coppell, and was silent for what seemed a long time. Then: 'Go on.'

'Why should anyone try to impersonate me – except to take my place?' Roger asked.

'I've got that far,' said Coppell.

'If they think I'm dead, if we can catch the man who's impersonating me, I might be able to impersonate *him*,' Roger said, softly. 'If I could spend even twenty-four hours as this other man who knows what I might find out.'

There was a pause; a much longer pause than before, with Coppell's heavy breathing coming clearly over the wire. Then at last Coppell growled:

'Won't help to find anything out if you're murdered before you can tell us what it is, will it?'

12

Intensive Care

ROGER LET THE Commander's words hang in the air for a few minutes. He was sure that Coppell was simply coping with his conscience, rather than experiencing aversion to the idea. He, Roger, was seeing more and more angles of it with almost every second; some good, some alarming. For instance if someone had planned to impersonate him, Roger, then what about Janet? For a short-term impersonation she probably didn't matter, but if someone wanted to act as Roger West for any length of time, even over a period of a few weeks, Janet would either have to go away or—

Be killed.

Murder?

Whenever these plans had been laid, Martin had been in Australia, the planners had no need to think there was any danger of discovery except from Janet.

Why was he thinking in terms of a long period?

He knew perfectly well, of course, even though he had not yet admitted it. Everyone knew crime was rising, fast. Everyone was thinking in simple terms: more criminals, a permissive, amoral society, more money, more rich people, more opportunity to steal. Even the crime of violence for its own sake was accepted by many as normal. Wars had bred into most races the acceptance of violence. And violence begat violence.

No one looked for any other explanation than normal growth within a changing society, except: Marriott.

And, be honest: except him, Roger West.

There might be many others, too, who had nothing on which to focus their half-formed theories, but – he had something to focus on. He—

'Handsome,' Coppell said, his patience exhausted, 'the Commissioner and I are both coming to see you. We shall come separately and should be there in about an hour. Don't run away.'

Roger laughed. 'No, sir.'

He rang off, and wiped a beading of sweat off his forehead. He should have realised Coppell was on another line to Trevillion; it wasn't in the man's nature to be patient, but he couldn't be taking this more seriously nor be more aware of the value of secrecy. Roger lay back, thinking more about Janet and Martin than about the case, then suddenly made up his mind, and called his home number. Janet answered so quickly that she must have been close by the telephone.

'This is Janet West.' Her voice was over-brisk; a frightened voice, because she had heard of the attacks on him. So, she was afraid. He heard the extension receiver move – so Martin was at the other telephone.

'Whatever you do,' he said, 'keep your voices down.'

Janet cried: '*Roger!*' as if her whole heart was in her voice; and on the instant Martin said 'Hush, Mum.'

'*Roger, you're safe,*' Janet breathed.

'I'm safe and not badly hurt,' Roger said, 'but you

may hear a lot of stories, even that I'm dead. Don't believe them but try to look as if you do.'

'You always *did* expect the impossible,' Janet said in a more normal voice.

'And get it,' Martin said.

'Just ignore anything in the newspapers, on television, or radio – even the evidence of your own ears and eyes,' Roger urged, and before either of them could make any other comment, he asked: 'Did you get those photographs, Martin?'

'Yes – and they're very good, though I say it as shouldn't.'

'Where's our set?'

'Mixed up among my paintings; I thought that was safest.'

'Good! Now, put them in a packet, bring a big handbag for them, Jan, and both come and see me here at St. George's Hospital. Look anxious coming in and unhappy when you leave. They'll allow you ten minutes here at most – I'll fix it beforehand. And if you can come right away you might just miss Coppell.' He heard Janet exclaim, and then he added, 'Look as if I'm at death's door, darling!'

'Oh, you *fool*,' breathed Janet, but tears muffled her voice.

*　　*　　*

Roger telephoned the Matron of his floor to be told that she had already had orders to say that he was in the intensive care unit; she told him that at least thirty newspapermen were in the street at Hyde Park Corner and that police had been drafted to all entrances, to make sure that no one could sneak into his ward.

Newspapermen? Roger wondered. Or assassins?
Why did they want to kill him?

Then Janet and Martin arrived, Janet tearful from emotional strain, Martin justly proud of his photographs. They had ten minutes and so little chance to talk. Before she left, Janet said:

'You will call me when you can, won't you?'

'I'll call you,' he promised. 'And if you ever get a message from a man who calls himself Brown Dog, that will be from me.'

She held him tightly but did not utter another word before turning and hurrying out, while Martin gave a farewell wave and muttered: 'Good luck, Dad,' as he followed her.

Roger lay back on his pillows, breathing hard; seeing them, trying to pretend there was nothing to worry about, had taken a lot out of him, and he needed no telling that he would not be fit this day, if for several days, for much exertion. He wiped his forehead and upper lip with a paper handkerchief, then pushed one pillow away and lay flat, closing his eyes. If he were asleep when Coppell and Trevillion came that wouldn't matter; half-an-hour's complete relaxation would give a needed edge to his mind.

He dozed off.

*   *   *

Janet and Martin walked along the hospital corridor, and they did not have to pretend to look pale or distressed. The apparent indifference of all the people they passed somehow hurt. Janet's face was set, and Martin had the sense to realise that this was no time to utter soothing phrases or put his arm round her shoulders. In the hallway, a man in a lounge suit said:

'There are fewer reporters this side, Mrs West.'

'Thank you.'

He led them along several passages to the entrance where the ambulances came, and the casualty patients. A dozen or more reporters and cameramen drew near. Questions were hurled, flashlights flicked brightly.

'How is he, Mrs West?'

'Is it true he was shot three times?'

'Are you sending for your other son, what's his name?'

Another man called: 'Richard. *Are* you sending for Richard?'

'Mr West, why did you come back from Australia when you did?'

'Was there some special reason? Did you know your father was working on a particularly dangerous job?'

'*Is he dying, Mrs West?*'

All of the time of this bombardment they were being escorted by several policemen towards a waiting car – a police limousine used only for V.I.P.s. The last question with all its cold-bloodedness, was uttered by a biggish, middle-aged man.

'For that, I ought to break your neck.' Martin uttered the first words either of them had spoken since the questions had started and the cameras flashed.

'I'd like to see you try,' the man retorted, half-sneering.

'Mr West—' began the nearest policeman.

Martin stopped in front of the man, looked him up and down, and said in a cold and angry voice: 'You are an unpleasant swine and a disgrace to your profession.'

'Why, you—' The man's fists came up, clenched, Janet cried: 'Martin!' Martin side-stepped a swing to the jaw and drove his own fists *one-two-three* with terrific power into the man's unprotected stomach. He staggered, then fell forward onto his knees, his face purple. Martin turned after his mother. No one else called out and no policeman spoke, but cameras clicked and flashed. First Janet, then Martin, got into the car, and the police driver got in, another officer beside him. This man was tall and fair-complexioned, with silvery hair.

'Martin,' Janet said, 'you shouldn't have done it.'

Martin grinned. 'I know I shouldn't but I'm glad I did.'

Silently they headed back for Chelsea, Martin's big hand now closed over his mother's. As they drew close to Bell Street, the man next to the driver turned his head, and said: 'I hope you won't take offence, Mrs. West, or you, sir, but I had orders to make one thing *very* clear to you.'

'What is it?' asked Janet.

'Absolute secrecy, about Mr West's true condition,' the man went on. 'You have a young lady staying temporarily at the house, haven't you?'

'Yes,' Janet answered.

'Don't say a word to her, whatever you do,' went on the policeman, and no one could have sounded more grave. 'You know how clever these newspaper chaps are at doing their job – they can get information out of a stone, sometimes. You two have some knowledge of how to deal with them—'

'I'll say!' exclaimed the driver, and then added quickly: 'Sorry, sir.'

'But this young lady, presumably, has had no

experience,' the man with the silvery hair said with great emphasis. 'It's absolutely vital no one breathes a word to her.'

'We won't,' Janet said.

'And you, Mr West?' the older man insisted.

'I won't,' Martin assured him, and then leaned forward in his seat and asked: 'Do you mind showing me your card?'

The driver stifled a snort of laughter.

The silvery-haired man turned in his seat. 'I'm Chief Superintendent Matthew Trannion,' he declared with saintly reproach, and handed Martin his card, which was countersigned both by Coppell and by the Commissioner. 'I hope you will take the most thorough precautions,' he went on. 'We don't really know what is happening but we are extremely worried. You will be guarded at Bell Street and wherever you go.'

They stopped, outside the Bell Street house. A plain-clothes man was at a window-cleaning cart a little way along, and nearby was a Television, Radio and Tape Recorder van.

Inside, Janet said: 'Martin, I don't think I've ever been more frightened. Thank *God* you're home.'

'It almost convinces you there is a God – a guiding hand, anyway,' Martin reflected. Then his voice brightened and he opened the front door. 'The worst thing about this affair is not being able to tell Anne.'

He thrust the door wide open – and Anne stood at the foot of the stairs. There was no way of telling whether she had heard what he said.

*   *   *

Only a few miles away, in St. George's Hospital, a

woman was saying into an internal telephone: 'I don't know whether we ought to wake him, Matron. I really don't want to do it on my own authority.'

'I'll talk to Dr. Lobb,' the Matron promised.

All of this was going on while Coppell kicked his heels in the waiting-room, knowing that it was no use talking to the staff here as he would have talked to the men at the Yard. He had received no word when Trevillion was ushered in. He gave a fierce grin.

'Makes me feel I'm breaking into the girls' dorm,' he remarked. 'Just arrived?'

'Ten minutes ago.'

'I hope he's not worse,' said Trevillion, and the expression on Coppell's face made it obvious that the idea had not occurred to him. Almost on that instant a man in a white coat came along the passage.

'Admiral Trevillion?' he smiled. 'I was a junior lieutenant under you once, sir. Armed. Mr Coppell? The staff were reluctant to wake Mr West, who has been given a fairly strong sedative, but he is conscious now – awake, I mean! – and quite able to talk. But it will be a day or two before he's on his feet again. He had quite a day.' Already, he was leading the way. 'My name is Lobb, by the way – Dr Lobb. We've had him removed as you requested to a single ward in an intensive care unit, and all the staff who have anything to do with him can be trusted absolutely.'

'You're very good,' said Trevillion. 'Which ship, doctor?'

'The *Rodney*, sir.'

'Ah. We must have a talk. Now—' They went into a lift, up two flights, along more passages which had the all-pervasive odour of strong antiseptics. Only one man, apparently an orderly, was with them.

'Three doors along,' Lobb said, turning to the right.

They were halfway there when the 'orderly' quickened his pace to a run and reached the third door. Thrusting it open, he rushed inside.

Before he disappeared, the others saw the gun in his hand.

13

The Fourth Attack

ROGER, WAKENED ONLY a few minutes before by a nurse who obviously disapproved, was sitting up, banked by pillows, feeling heavy-headed but on the whole much better. He was in a different room, with an oxygen cylinder and other apparatus he didn't recognise, and was girding himself to deal with the two great men. Then he heard a sharp sound of footsteps, a bellow which could only come from Trevillion, a roar of '*Stop him*!' from Coppell. He needed no more telling what had happened, and his reflexes had never been better. He flung a glass of orange juice towards the door as it began to open, and rolled off the bed. For a sickening moment he thought he would hit his left arm; worse, that the orange juice had landed on Trevillion's face.

Beneath the high bed he saw feet.

The feet of a small man, and suddenly his hands and face as he crouched down to shoot beneath the bed. The feet of a big man, enormous feet – Coppell's. Coppell drew back his right leg and kicked the crouching man with such force that the gun slithered from his grasp. Then small, well-shod feet – Trevillion's? No, the doctor, bending down and

picking up the gun, while Coppell and Trevillion lifted
the assailant clear of the floor.

Coppell called: 'Are you all right, West?'

'West!' roared Trevillion.

'Worse for wear but all right,' Roger said. He hauled
himself to his feet and then two nurses and three
policemen came hurrying in, and Roger allowed
himself to be half-lifted onto the bed, pillows placed
behind his shoulders. Coppell's voice came, subdued to
the tone he considered suitable for a hospital.

'Take this man out, handcuff him, take him to the
Yard, get all the details you can about him. I'll charge
him with attempted murder when I get back.'

Roger watched the man.

He was smaller than average but otherwise looked
normal enough; fair-haired, blue-eyed, pleasant-look-
ing. He made no attempt to struggle with the odds so
heavily against him, but allowed himself to be hand-
cuffed to a police officer. The three of them went out.
Roger looked from one to the other of his visitors, and
said: 'I daresay I could lay on some tea, gentlemen.'

'Easily,' declared a nurse, from the door.

'Thank you,' said Trevillion, in his attractively gruff
voice. 'For three, eh, Commander.' His beetling brows
rose over eyes which held a twinkle. He laid a gentle
hand on West's shoulder. 'Five more, eh?'

'I'd rather not use them all up today,' said Roger.

'What the hel- heck are you talking about?' Coppell
demanded.

'Lives,' Roger said.

'Lives? What – oh, lives. Four attempts to kill you
today and five to come.' He guffawed. The others
smiled, and the two senior police officials pulled up
chairs.

They did not speak for a few moments, but they became much more sober. Two or three people walked past outside, before Trevillion asked: 'Like to postpone this discussion, West?'

'Why should I, sir?'

'Get a good night's rest before we get down to the hard core of the situation.'

'I need to know some of the circumstances before I answer,' Roger said. 'One key point, anyhow. Am I still under suspicion?'

'No,' stated Trevillion, flatly.

Roger's heart leapt.

'Apart from the thickness and curl of the hair there were other points of difference which showed up under a magnifier which enlarged all features and blemishes one hundred times,' went on Trevillion. 'We've had our experts as well as consultants on this for hours. You are completely in the clear, West. Isn't that right, Commander?'

'Glad to say it is.'

Roger felt as if the world were once again a pleasant place to live in. He had not realised, until now that it was lifted, how very much the weight of suspicion had crushed his spirit.

'Then I'd like to hear everything,' he said at last.

'Excellent, excellent!' enthused Trevillion. 'Commander, you know all the details. Go ahead.'

Coppell looked pleasantly surprised, but had the wit to say: 'Sure, sir?'

'Yes. Get on with it, man.'

'Right!' boomed Coppell. He paused for a moment, as if suddenly aware that he had spoken too loudly; then scarcely able to disguise his excitement, he went on: 'We caught the man who shot at you.'

'And followed the would-be assassins' taxi to an address in Lowndes Square,' put in Trevillion. 'One man who lives there is one of the most famous make-up artists in Europe. Another is a prominent Polish plastic surgeon – a man of real genius.' He broke off and looked at Coppell, as if commanding him to speak next.

'The third one, who seems to matter most, is Hunter,' Coppell said gruffly. 'Rake Hunter.'

Roger hitched himself up on his pillows, looked from one man to the other, and said in a low-pitched voice: 'I shall wake up in a minute.'

'You're awake already,' said Coppell. 'You've *been* asleep, just like the rest of us, that's the trouble. A brilliant make-up artist, a bloody good plastic surgeon, and the biggest fence in England with international contacts all over the world. *That's* what we've got on our hands, Handsome. Unlikely as it may seem we've got a pretty good idea that some of our personnel may have been impersonated. Mostly detective officers, one or two sergeants from the uniformed branch. Now supposing they were injected with some drug which causes amnesia, then impersonated at a place and time which made a certain crime easy, and after that, released. *They* wouldn't remember anything. Four separate cases of dereliction of duty came up recently for disciplinary action: one man was suspended, three reprimanded for neglect of duty and reduced to the ranks.'

Roger thought almost wildly: Yes, yes, do get on with it!

'There were three instances of officers on special guard or surveillance duty who were drunk on their job – and they enabled the crimes to be committed also. Two were allowed to retire at the rank they held, one was suspended.'

'Yes, yes, yes!' breathed Roger.

'And there were even more serious cases,' Coppell went on ponderously. 'Men who broke into banks, stores, post offices and shops, and stole substantial sums in money or in kind. Know how many men we've drummed out of the Force, West?'

'Too many,' Roger said hoarsely. 'Far too many.'

'Right! But we all put it down to today's conditions.'

'Things certainly aren't like they used to be,' Trevillion complained, rather like a comedian chorus.

Roger nodded agreement. 'All the same, sir,' he said slowly, 'it still wasn't a *wild* proportion. We – most of us at Superintendent level, that is – thought it was just a case of the rotten apples falling from the tree.'

'We all did,' Coppell growled. 'But impersonation within the Force would certainly explain some of this peculiar behaviour that has been going on. And it would tie in with the fact that they had a go at fixing someone to take *your* place. Don't ask me why they're so anxious to kill you now. Something you've done, or said, has put the wind up them.'

'Hunter,' Roger said with emphasis.

'Need you keep repeating yourself?' demanded the Admiral, but his testiness was forced.

'Always said to be like me,' Roger went on, gruffly.

Neither of the others spoke.

'And probably the man in that photograph,' Roger went on.

'Damn near certain to be,' Coppell declared.

'And he was going to impersonate me to pull off some big coup.'

'It seems like it.'

'Do either of you have the faintest idea *what* coup?' demanded Trevillion. 'I may not have been a policeman for long, I may not be a policeman at all, but I do know something very big would have to justify such a risk as that.'

'There doesn't have to be one job,' argued Roger. 'Looking like me and carrying my credentials he could get almost anywhere in London. And if I had two or three men with me supposed to be police officers—'

'He *must* have had a big coup in mind,' insisted Trevillion.

'Don't see that it matters much,' broke in Coppell. 'They want him dead so they aren't going to use him.'

Trevillion didn't argue.

'And they want him dead very badly and urgently or they wouldn't have taken such chances,' added Coppell.

'Sir, as I said earlier – why don't I die?' Roger asked.

Trevillion made a sign which looked very much like the sign of the cross.

'They want me dead so it must be for a major purpose,' Roger went on. 'We've only to make an announcement to the Press and the whole country will know about it tonight, or at the latest tomorrow morning. Once they think they've got rid of me, then—' He gulped. 'For one thing, they'll relax for a while. Inevitable reaction, even for men of their calibre. Sure you know where they are?'

'No doubt, no shadow of doubt,' Trevillion declared, and then coughed, as if he had some difficulty in speaking.

'We know,' said Coppell.

'Can we pick him up?' asked Roger.

Neither of the others spoke, and he had no doubt at

all that in their minds was the idea which had come to him not long ago. A crazy idea. One which would almost certainly fail. Only a lunatic would think of it: or three lunatics.

'It could be done. Pick him up, I mean.'

'By himself.'

'There would have to be a way.'

'Yes,' Roger said softly. 'He would have to be by himself. It's essential nobody could betray the fact that we'd got him. And—'

'West!' barked Trevillion. 'I'm a man of plain words. What's on your mind?'

There was a dead silence as both he and Coppell gazed as if spellbound at Roger.

He gazed back, smiling faintly.

'Impersonating Hunter, sir,' he stated flatly.

Trevillion breathed: 'You would take that chance?'

'If we are to break up this group I don't see how we can do it, except from the inside,' Roger said, but although he spoke easily enough his nerves were tense and his heart was racing. Of course, it was true. Hoist the group with their own petard. It wasn't even an original idea but—

What would they do if they discovered the deception?

Coppell was looking at him very intently. Trevillion was breathing hard and noisily. Roger leaned to the bedside table and took up the packet of photographs which Martin had given him. He opened it, ripping the plastic tape off the brown paper in his impatience, and then began to riffle through picture after picture. They could hardly have been better, and he explained them in the same detail that Marriott had explained them to him. But he was doing it mechanically, half of his thoughts being of the task for which he had volunteered, and its dangers; of the effect on Janet, even on the boys. Perhaps it was a good thing that pretty Anne Claire had come along just now, to take Martin's mind off the main preoccupation and perhaps even help his mother.

Could they maintain the pretence that he was dead? Or was that really asking too much of them?

He smiled faintly. They would manage.

'West,' said Trevillion, turning over the last photograph, after Roger had fallen silent for at least a minute. 'Our general feeling has been of a sharp rise in crime.'

Roger nodded. 'I know, sir.'

'If there have been these impersonations on a large scale then this could be the explanation.'

They all knew it; why keep on repeating it?

'Yes, sir,' Roger said.

'So if we can break up this particular organisation we might see a reverse trend in crime of every kind.'

'It's very likely,' Roger said. 'We mustn't forget—'

'Mustn't forget that a lot of crime's imitative,'Coppell put in, importantly. 'The *whole* rise in the crime rate isn't due to this group. It sets the pace and others follow. Talking to your friend Appleby this afternoon,' he went on. 'Appleby's opinion is that many of the crimes of violence, murder with sex perversion, etc., are imitative. There's a sudden wave of crime, everyone gets away with it, so these sex nuts blow their tops.'

He wasn't exactly quoting Appleby but Roger could almost hear the pathologist saying these things in his own words.

'The reverse would apply,' Roger said. 'Make some

big captures, clamp down on it hard, and the rate should fall. There's one thing you may have overlooked, gentlemen.'

'What?' barked Trevillion.

'I don't think I've overlooked much,' said Coppell, aggressively defensive.

'If you pick Hunter up, by police regulations he has to be charged within twenty-four hours,' Roger pointed out. 'If I can get past the first twenty-four hours I may need a lot more time. It simply wouldn't be possible to do anything in a short period. Now can we get past that one?' he demanded of Coppell, for the Commander knew far more about police procedure and the demands of the law than Trevillion would ever know.

Coppell pursed his lips, but laughter lurked in his eyes.

'You can't get out of it that easy, Handsome. I'll fix that – *and* I'll have the basket up and ready for trial at the Assizes. That's not our problem; catching Hunter on his own is the one that's going to give me the headaches. But we'll switch it. Meanwhile – if you agree, sir,' he said with a sidelong glance at Trevillion, 'West had better stay at death's door until we know when we can pick Hunter up. And it's got to be quick and slick. Hunter leaves the house at some point, a few hours later Handsome here goes back. Quick and *slick*,' he breathed again.

'Do you know,' said the Commissioner, his voice suddenly troubled, 'I am beginning to think it's too much to ask.'

14

Three Days' 'Rest'

HE MEANT WHAT he said. The sincerity showed in his eyes, in the way he pushed his chair back and walked across the room, then turned with his hands behind him; a pose he had struck a thousand times on the bridges of the ships he had commanded. His square shoulders, his full chest, the flatness of his waist, might have been those of a much younger man.

'I am beginning to *feel* that it is too much to ask,' he said in a deep voice which yet carried only to the four corners of the room.

'Surely – er – surely that's up to West,' Coppell said, unable to stop himself from sounding disappointed.

'It is not. It is up to me,' rasped Trevillion, looking at Roger. 'You should at least have three or four days to think about this.'

'Sir,' Roger said, 'can you count on the fingers of your two hands the number of men you've sent out on suicide missions?'

'No, I'm damned if I can! But the navy—'

'Have none come back?'

'Of course some of them have come back.'

'With respect, sir, we're on a mission as important as nine out of ten of the suicide missions you've authorised, and I don't think anyone would question the need. But I do ask for two or three days' grace.'

'What for?' demanded Coppell; it was almost a crow of delight.

'To get thoroughly fit. To be able to use this arm reasonably well. And to swot up on Hunter. I need to know everything there is to know about that man – not just his criminal record. Two or three newspapers have done articles on him – wasn't there a book which no publisher would handle, it was too hot on the sex and drugs angle? I need a copy of that. And I need to know as much about his early life as I can, and his girl friends – hasn't he been married four times – and children, relatives, and what they look like. And I need to know his favourite phrases – he likes to be with it – and the kind of films he likes to see, his favourite television programmes.'

'You need a week,' Coppell said.

'Get me the information and I'll have it in my head in three days,' Roger assured him. 'Are you in agreement, sir?' he asked Trevillion.

'I am,' Trevillion said, 'and now I honestly believe that you will be one of those who come back.'

*　　*　　*

The information about Rake Hunter poured in.

The chief source was the book, a typescript of which was found in a journalist's rooms, 'Waiting,' he said, 'until an age became permissive enough to allow its publication.' It was exhaustive; going back to Hunter's childhood it thus gave Roger one of his best breaks.

Hunter's mother and father and only sister had died in an air raid over London in 1942, and he had few relatives. He had, however, dozens, hundreds, of friends, four ex-wives, and an unguessable number of mistresses. He was generous with them; if there was a good side to his character it was his generosity. But what he expected of them was, both vulgarly and factually, the limit. A great deal was suspected of his criminal activities – and again he paid well for all services. He ran a protection racket in Soho and in various cities, was behind most of the drug pushing in England, and had a system by which he could send couriers by air, at any hour of day or night, to deliver stolen jewels and securities thousands of miles from the point of their theft.

He was merciless.

If a man or woman cheated him he maimed, disfigured, or killed them.

The extent of his activities had never been fully understood in England, but there had been rumours and a certain amount of information, which had filtered through from various continental cities. He was nicknamed 'Rake' because of his reputation with women, and was known in most capitals of the world. That he had shown up in England, was something quite new.

Roger read every word he could about the man, and studied every photograph.

Facially, the resemblance was quite remarkable. There was, too, a similarity in the square, broad shoulders and deep chest. No fully naked photographs were available so there was no way of telling what birthmarks he might have. His thighs were thinner than Roger's and his calves were not quite so well-shaped, but only someone who knew him with the closest intimacy would notice that.

His mannerisms were difficult to pick up; few whom the police talked to knew him well enough to describe them. His voice was another problem; there were many who had heard it but there was no tape. This was going to be the greatest problem and so the greatest danger.

'You can have a cold,' Coppell suggested.

'Caught and sounding in my voice in an hour or two?'

'Well, come up with a better idea,' Coppell suggested sourly.

They were on the telephone, Coppell as always using his private line, and rain was pounding against the window, driven by great gusts. Roger didn't answer for a few moments and ever-impatient Coppell growled: 'Okay, take your time.'

'I think I know a way we might get by,' Roger said. 'Do you remember Captain Frost of the Homicide Branch of the New York Police?'

'That friend of yours, yes.'

'Telephone him,' urged Roger. 'Don't mention me as being above ground, but find out if he can put his hands on a tape of Hunter's voice. I think they had him in for questioning a few years ago and if they took a tape, they wouldn't have thrown it away.'

'Right – but damn it, West, it's three o'clock in the morning in New York!'

'His home number's in my desk file,' Roger said. 'He won't mind being woken up. Try not to speak to his wife, though.'

*   *   *

In fact, Frost's wife didn't wake.

'Yes,' he said. 'We took a tape and we can take a

copy and fly it right over. If this will help Handsome—'

'It will help avenge him, anyhow,' Coppell said.

The American seemed to catch his breath.

'So it's really as bad as that.'

'I wish to God it wasn't.'

'And you want all you can get on Rake Hunter?'

'Every little bit, every crumb,' Coppell said.

'I hear you,' said the American, 'and I can help you. I'll send this tape over with one of our policewomen. She's quite a doll. She would be more of a doll if she didn't have barbed-wire scars on her right cheek. She lived for a month with Hunter, she went that far to get him, but he found out. There's a woman who would give her right hand to see Hunter where he should be. You can rely on her absolutely.'

Coppell's face held the awe of thanksgiving as he put the telephone down.

*   *   *

Lieutenant Maria Consuela, of the New York Police Department was due to arrive, with Coppell, at any time. Roger, sitting up in an easy chair, but still in a dressing gown, wondered what she would really be like and whether Coppell's hopefulness would be justified. One thing was certain: Ivan Frost, his New York friend, and the one he knew better than most, certainly would not send anyone unless she was good. But Ivan didn't really know the situation. He, Roger, might have been wiser to talk to him himself. But one couldn't have a private line to New York and those lines could be the eyes and ears of the world.

He thought he had everything else he needed except the voice and some of those personal habits a man never lost; crooking a finger, playing with a lip, an ear, scratching one's nose – there were dozens of little things. He had once recognised and arrested a badly-wanted criminal simply by recognising his mannerism of rubbing his right elbow with his left hand.

Footsteps sounded – one set heavy, one set light.

Coppell, and Maria Consuela.

Coppell gave his customary heavy bang on the door and then opened it, but he didn't come in first. He stood aside, letting his companion precede him. A hardened policeman he was, nevertheless, aghast at the havoc wreaked on Maria Consuela's beauty; and concerned at the effect of this havoc on Roger. Because of the particular situation of the door, and the fact that his chair was behind the bed, Roger saw her profile first; an unblemished and quite superbly beautiful profile.

She was Spanish, of course; or Mexican.

Her hair was raven black and her complexion so much the colour of a peach it seemed unnatural.

Roger stood up as she turned full face towards him.

Had a tiger clawed her from just beneath the eye down to the side of the mouth the effect could not have been more disfiguring. It actually twisted one side of her lip a little so that it was almost set in a permanent sneer. With the terrible knowledge of how he would be affected, she stopped just inside the room, waiting.

*   *   *

Maria Consuela thought: It is not possible, they are so alike.

She waited and watched and she thought: He will get used to it, like all the others.

She was aware that his gaze strayed from her scar to

her eyes, then he smiled and moved towards the foot of the bed, while she gasped: 'The smile is uncanny! I could swear you were Rake Hunter.'

* * *

Roger had a confusion of thoughts as he looked at her, and the last comment did not, at first, have full effect. But for that scar she was quite remarkably beautiful, and she had – well, she had a figure most women would envy. But the most beautiful thing about her were her eyes.

They drew close enough to shake hands, and he said: 'Thank God they didn't touch your eyes.'

'Rake wouldn't do that,' she said. 'If he blinded me I wouldn't be able to see myself.'

'Still so bitter?' Roger asked.

'Until my dying day.'

He was still holding her hand.

'I hope not,' he said. 'I hope very much that you're wrong.' They stared at each other for what seemed a long time, and he was not, then, aware of the door closing; not until afterwards did he realise that Coppell had sensed, in one of his rare moments of perception, that they would get on better without him. Roger realised he still held her hand; he released it and motioned to an armchair opposite his. 'Do sit down.'

She continued to stand.

'Why should it matter so much to you whether I am bitter or not?'

'I've seen a lot of human beings,' Roger said. 'Plain and homely, old and young, bright and lovely. The worst thing that can happen to any of them is to be filled with bitterness.'

'Don't you mean hatred?'

'No,' he replied. 'Bitterness. They can be half-brothers but they're not the same. Hatred can drive a man to extreme effort, to passion, to fury – but bitterness withers him. It's like growing old inside while looking young outside.'

At last she sat down.

'Tell me, are you really going to impersonate Rake Hunter?'

'Did they tell you that?'

'They had to make me realise how important it was that you learned all you could about him. All the little intimacies. All the little mannerisms. Did they tell you he has a new wife?'

He caught his breath.

'No.'

'She's just learning.'

Roger said again: 'No. No, that was the one thing I hadn't thought of.'

'Sleeping with his wife or lovers,' she said.

When he didn't speak she went on: 'Unless you're prepared to play the part absolutely, don't go. You couldn't possibly win, and it would be sheer waste if you went, knowing in advance that you were going to lose. Wouldn't it?' When he didn't answer she pulled herself to her feet.

'Roger West,' she said, clearly, '*listen*. This man is a devil. What he's done to me is nothing compared with what he's done to others. He has a world-wide criminal organisation and when he can't buy his way into the police forces, he works as he's working here in London, against you. Catch him. Hang him or put him away for life, and you will have done more for society than in all the rest of your police work put together.'

She gripped his hands so tightly that his fingers hurt.
'What are you going to do? Let those conventions
you live by, let faithfulness to your pretty little wife or
some half-understood religious covenant stop you? Or
are you going to take a chance of doing what no man
has ever been able to do? *Break Rake Hunter's power.*'

15

Tension of Waiting

ROGER WEST, HEARING the passion in her voice, became increasingly aware of her – as a woman and a beautiful one, rather than as a colleague. He had been, to a lesser extent, from the moment she entered the room.

'Such hate and bitterness,' he said again. 'Tell me.'

She did not answer and he did not speak again, waiting, sure that eventually she would answer. And indeed, she said:

'I was in love. With – a good man. He wanted me to leave the Police Force and stay at home. Sometimes, I – I thought I wanted to. And finally I decided to. He was a stockbroker, a Presbyterian, a—' She broke off, and then went on again: 'Not smug. *Good.* Then I was assigned to Hunter and there was only one way for a woman cop to deal with him. I told myself I was doing as much good as Jeremy, in a different way. Even a lot more. It was going to be my last job with the police.'

She paused, but it was not time for him to speak. Was it time for him to kiss her, very lightly, on the cheek and on the eyes, tasting the salt of her tears? She showed no sign that she knew what he was thinking, but suddenly she went on:

'Then, this happened. One of the newspapers got a

picture of me just afterwards, called me one of
Hunter's molls. The Police Department couldn't
protect me – I'd known that from the beginning. They
took me to hospital in a police ambulance, and all New
York knew where I was.' She paused. 'But— Jeremy
didn't come.

'He didn't come then and he didn't come
afterwards. I've never seen him again. I had a stiff note
saying he was sure I would understand why he couldn't
go on. A year – less than a year later, he married.'

There was a tap at the door which began to open
and Roger called out: 'Can we have some tea in half-an-
hour?' and the caller closed the door on a quiet: 'Yes,
Mr. West.'

Maria Consuela forced a smile.

'I could fall in love with you at the crook of your little
finger,' she said, lightly daring.

'I shall keep that little finger absolutely rigid until
we have Hunter where we want him,' he answered,
just as lightly. 'After that I make no promises. Maria.'

'Yes?'

'Did Coppell tell you what I need?'

'Yes – but not in detail.'

'First, the tape, and try to imitate Hunter's voice,'
he said. 'I want to listen to it half-a-dozen times and
then talk with you as if I were he. Your job's to tell me
where and when I miss. You don't have to be a speech
therapist – I don't have to be absolutely right all the
time but I must get the basic vowels and any speech
mannerisms. Did he lisp? *Does* he lisp?'

'No. But he sometimes squeaks.'

'Squeaks?'

'When he gets excited. Shouldn't we use the tape?
It's in my purse.'

'Don't move! I'll get it.' He stretched for her bag, which had fallen from her chair, then watched with pleasure the neatness and competence of her hands as she searched for, and found, the tape.

Soon, a man began to speak. Roger did not need to ask if the voice was Hunter's, for it was unmistakably English, although some words and particularly some phrases were American. Such as: 'C'm on', instead of 'come on' and 'waal' for 'well' and 'you're telling me, friend', or 'you can't fool this baby'. He was giving instructions to a group of men and there seemed to be one or two women in the party, but no one spoke much, then usually in monosyllables. Finally, he said: 'Okay, what are you waiting for?' and there was a scraping of chairs followed, almost unbelievably, by the first movement of 'Swan Lake'.

'That did surprise you, didn't it?' Maria laughed.

'Does he go in for the classics?'

'He had about twelve records,' she answered, 'but nobody makes the mistake of asking for any one of them by name. He doesn't know the names. He'll say: 'Let's have the one about the swans, baby'. Or else: 'That V for Victory, how does it go now?' And he is always off key.'

'Up or down?'

'There's no set rule.'

'I am thankful for small mercies! Shall we hear the tape again and then you ask me what I know about his music loves and his phrases. Tea will soon be here.'

'The British panacea,' she said, without moving. 'And as I am a Latin, and reputed to be passionate, suppose I enliven this so dry discussion by creating a scene, one worthy in every sense of a Latin? Then when tea comes the nurses would be shocked. Being English, they would probably run screaming. And that would bring the newspapermen and the photographers. And what a scandal you would have on your hands. You'd never live it down.'

Roger said drily: 'Even for an American you have a peculiar idea of the English.'

'Let me dream,' she pleaded. A little alarmed, not knowing whether she was serious, or being amused at his expense, he heard, with a surge of relief, the clink of crockery. A perfunctory tap, and a trolley laden with a silver plated tea-set and some minute cakes, all very V.I.P., was pushed in.

'Would you believe this,' Maria said in the brightest of voices, 'this is the first time I've *ever* had tea English style.'

'Then how on earth have you had it?' asked the smaller of the two trim-looking nurses.

'Iced,' she answered.

'Iced!' breathed the others as if touched with horror.

That was the moment when Coppell looked in. Was everything going all right, he asked breezily. What were the chances of catching Hunter in the next few days. Apparently the fellow had met and become enamoured of a red-haired girl and they had been out three nights in a row. If the affair prospered. . .

'I'll need at least two days,' Roger said.

'He'll be word perfect in two days,' said Maria Consuela. 'But there is a problem, Commander.'

'Made to be solved,' replied Coppell smugly. 'What is it?'

'We should be in a hotel suite not in a hospital,' Maria declared. 'Roger is probably used to it by now but this place does rather reek of antiseptics. He needs a Turkish bath or a sauna, it doesn't matter which, and a suit of clothes which Hunter would wear, ties, socks, shoes—'

'We can get all of those,' Coppell said. 'Trannion has done a remarkable job, Handsome. He's found Hunter's cleaners who have 'lost' a couple of suits, and his laundry, even his shoe-repairers.' He was obviously elated. 'But I do think Lieutenant Consuela is right, you can't stay here any longer.'

'When I leave here,' Roger said, soberly, 'I am supposed to be a corpse.'

Coppell grimaced and went to the window. There was a dark shadow in the room, not caused only by the heavy clouds and the rain outside.

'Yes,' Coppell said at last. 'Trannion and Partridge with the hospital authorities have arranged that. I don't know whether you want the details.'

He obviously hoped Roger didn't but Roger answered: 'Please.'

'Right. It can be tonight or tomorrow night. An unidentified body will be placed in a coffin and will be officially you. Press, friends, your wife, will be informed. Your wife does know the truth, of course. There will be a simple ceremony planned for the Hampstead Crematorium. You, meanwhile, will be removed in a linen basket to a small hotel – one of those we run. Only those already in the secret will know you are there. You and Lieutenant Consuela can have communicating-rooms, of course. Once you are both satisfied that you can play his part, Handsome, he will be picked up at the night club he chooses to visit that night. He will be called to the telephone, leaving the redhead at the table alone – unless she chooses to run to the powder room. The switch will be made at the night club. O'Malley will be in charge of the operation and I haven't any doubt at all that it will go smoothly – up to that point.'

He paused. He drew a deep breath. And then he said gratingly: 'After that, it's up to you. We need absolutely convincing evidence of what happens at the house in Lowndes Square, what arrangements are made for theft and distribution of the jewels and currency – in fact, we want the place broken open so that we can walk in and take them all.' He paused again.

'But—

'It will take days and it might take weeks.'

*   *   *

'Give me those two more days, away from here, and I'll be ready,' Roger said.

*   *   *

From his point of view, from Maria Consuela's, from the point of view of the police, everything went perfectly. The transfer to the small hotel, one of several run in London by the police when it was necessary to have visiting policemen and other celebrities accommodated, was pleasant, comfortable, and had good English food. Their waiter, waitress and chambermaid were all well-trusted Yard employees.

If Roger had an anxiety, it was for Janet. For the newspapers screamed the news of his death, reporters besieged her and, if he knew Richard, Richard would come flying home from wherever he was on location. When it was all over, when he was found to be alive. . .

But would he ever return to life?

*   *   *

'Are you absolutely sure?' stormed Richard. 'Supposing they're lying? And supposing he walks into a trap? My *God,* it's wicked. That's what it is, it's diabolical. I know what I'm going to do. I'm going to see Coppell in the morning. No, dammit, not that flat-footed oaf, I'm going to see Trevillion. And I'll threaten them with all the glare of publicity television can give, and believe me, that's plenty! I won't stand for it!'

'Richard, please,' begged his mother.

'Stop talking a lot of tommy-rot,' Martin said, calmly. 'Dad knew what he was letting himself in for. The police will get the real Rake Hunter and Dad will take his place. He may only need a few hours to get the information. Calm down, and – hush!'

All three sat absolutely silent, and the front door closed; Anne Claire had just come in. Richard hadn't yet met her and she had no idea that he had flown home that afternoon.

'Don't breathe a word to her, understand?' Martin ordered.

'*Must* we see her tonight?' asked Richard, moodily. 'I don't mind that she's got my room, but if we have to talk in whispers it's a hell of a situation.'

'We must say hallo,' Janet declared. 'We always do.' She crossed to the door and opened it, calling Anne, who was already halfway up the stairs, She stood indeterminate, obviously not sure whether she should intrude on a family crisis of this kind.

Janet thought: She's the most considerate child.

Martin thought: What *is* it about her I like?

Richard thought: And we can't even *talk*!

*   *   *

For Roger, it was utterly different, in every way, from anything he had experienced before. As he learned more about Hunter, about Pilaski the Polish plastic surgeon, about Cecil Smith the British make-up artist, the more he realised that it wasn't nearly enough. After the first day or two of confidence, a mood of fear had set in. He should have expected, but had not, the fear of being recognised the moment he stepped inside. Fear, especially, of Pilaski. Coppell on one of his visits, had let out some facts about Pilaski. That as a plastic surgeon he *was* a genius; and as a man who could disfigure and mutilate, at least as good.

In one way there wasn't enough time to learn all he had to learn.

In another, he had too much time, too much waiting.

Maria showed remarkable patience. She was the person who could tell him about these men; what angered them, for instance, and what Hunter would do, or not do, in his dealings with them.

He would never criticise, only praise, she said. Never say a change in a man's appearance was bad or poor, simply that this, or that or the other might possibly be improved.

And he would never utter a word of criticism about Poland to Akka Pilaski, not ever criticise or complain about the constant record-playing of Polish music. The Pole venerated Paderewski, for instance.

One never called Smith 'Smithy' or, in view of 'Cecil', Cissy. Always the full name Cecil with the accent on the 'e'. *Sessil.*

There were dozens, there were hundreds of these things.

And there was the layout of the house itself, learned from the architects' plans but, so far, no sure way of knowing which was Hunter's room. Of all the problems and the dangers this in many ways seemed the worst to Roger.

'I just don't see how I can fail to do something wrong as soon as I step into the house,' he said to Maria. He was sitting by a window where the Venetian blinds were drawn so that no one could possibly look up and, by chance, recognise him.

'Roger,' Maria said, 'the first night is the easiest.'

He almost shouted at her.

'How can you say that? I won't know right from left, I won't—'

'Let the redhead lead you,' Maria advised, and she came and stood over him; and then to his surprise knelt down in front of him. 'Listen,' she said. 'You don't even have to take her to bed that first night. You can pick a quarrel with her. He takes offence at the slightest thing.' She took his arm. 'Roger,' she went on, 'I think there's only one real danger. Only one thing that will give you away almost at once.'

'What's that?' he demanded, hoarsely.

'You're too tense. And in that mood you won't be able to put on his swagger, or look as if you own the world. For that's how he looks. You need to relax, my dear, if only you could.' She took his hands in her own, and now her voice held an edge of tension. 'Try it out on me. Break your self-imposed restraint for a little while. You'd be more disloyal to Janet by getting yourself killed than by a little experimental love-making. Stop thinking every minute, stop going over and over everything in your mind. It will work as smoothly as silk when you're there *if* you're rested.'

When he did not answer or move, she turned her face away, saying with a half-sigh: 'This isn't just duty for me, Roger. I think I've fallen in love with you.'

16

The Switch

HE WOKE, FEELING calmer and more clear-minded than he had for days.

He was alone in his room, and he wondered where Maria was, and smiled sleepily, dreamily, happily. She hadn't gone far; neither of them had been outside these two rooms for three full days. He stretched, yawned and remembered; and he remembered at least as vividly as everything else, her saying: 'This isn't just duty for me, Roger. I think I've fallen in love with you.'

And, heaven help him, he believed her.

She might have lied, simply because she was so sure he needed support and reassurance, but would he be very conceited if he thought she hadn't? It was half-past eleven – at night.

He placed his hands behind his head and decided to give her a few more minutes before calling out; and then he heard a movement and saw a shadow at the door; and, before she actually entered, the chink of china. Bless her! She had made tea. He had shown her twice, for they had an electric kettle and a hot plate, and she had made his tea at least as well as either of the boys could have made it.

She wore a turquoise silk dressing-gown embroidered with golden dragons; but for that scar she

146

would have been beautiful: damnation, she *was* beautiful. She paused for a moment, as if genuinely startled by his appearance and said clearly 'El Magnifico,' and then came and placed the tray on the bedside table.

'You are very beautiful,' he said. 'My mind is full of wishes.'

She made a mock salaam.

'The master is most generous.' She leaned forward and brushed his cheek with her lips. 'I thought I would have to wake you, and hated to.'

'Why should you have to?' he asked.

Before she answered, he knew what she was going to say. It was in her eyes: the news she had to break. She poured out tea, a little milk first, but no sugar, and then said equably:

'He has booked a table at the Moon Desert for one o'clock.'

'Well, well.' Roger took his cup, and drank thoughtfully. 'A table for two, eh.'

'Yes. They don't know who he's taking but the redhead is still at Lowndes Square.'

'Clara Defoe.'

'Called Clara Dee.'

'Who loves having the nape of her neck fingered and kissed.'

It was like repeating a well-learned lesson.

'Yes,' Maria answered. 'They'll – the police – will go for him at half-past one. They'll call for you at one o'clock.'

'Everything arranged,' he said. 'Maria.'

'Yes?'

'I feel a hundred times more sure of myself.'

'A man is a man,' she said.

'Maria—'

'Yes?'

'There are a thousand things I would like to say.'

'Not one,' she urged, and placed a finger against his lip. 'We've said everything we shall ever need to say. I'll run your bath.'

'With perfume of roses bath salts.'

'Naturally, Mr Hunter.'

'I hope he hasn't changed to tulips or—'

'They still supply him with perfume of roses from the shop in Audley Street.'

'You think of everything,' he said. 'As I sit in that bath I shall begin to change my personality. When I'm dressed in one of his suits I shall feel like Mr Hunter.'

'Well, you'd better hurry. You haven't too much time.'

'I'll be out in five minutes.'

Five minutes – into a bathroom filled with steam and the perfume of roses.

Fifty minutes and he was dressed except for his jacket, and he looked the same yet felt a different man. He drew the sleeve of his shirt up over the scar of the bullet wound and Maria placed first a very fine plastic plaster over it, and then sprayed it so that only on closest inspection could anyone see there was a scar. The only words she said were: 'It's a good thing it was on the inside of the arm.' She helped him on with his jacket.

He examined himself in a full length mirror, and said: 'It's almost a pity I have to change into whatever suit he's wearing tonight.'

'You might be lucky,' she said.

'Yes.' Roger held his hands out to her and gripped her but did not draw her to him. 'Maria, I shall come back.'

'Of course you will come back,' she said.

At that moment there was a tap at the door, and a man called out: 'Your car is here, sir.'

Roger bent down and kissed the ugly scars. A moment later he was out of the room, and a minute after that he was out of the hotel and getting into the car to take him to London's latest night spot.

His voice echoed.

'I shall come back. I shall come back. I shall come back.'

*　　*　　*

Maria Consuela watched as he got into the car, watched as the car drove off. When the red light turned the corner she moved away.

*　　*　　*

Roger wore a hat with the brim turned low over his eyes, and a scarf which muffled his chin. Men were waiting at the service entrance to the Moon Desert; there was an odour of grilled steak. At a door marked: 'Up' a man in plainclothes was standing.

'We've got him, sir.'

'Good.'

'There's a man at the top of these stairs to take you to the changing room.'

'Thanks.'

The man waiting was O'Malley, eager-eyed, with a single powerful handshake, and a gasped: 'My God, you're him to the life!'

'What suit's he wearing?'

'It's darker than that but we've got it off him.'

O'Malley looked down at Roger's shoes. 'The shoes will do.'

They crossed a narrow passage with several doors marked: 'Manager', 'Assistant Manager', 'Star Artist', 'Girls'. O'Malley pushed open the door of the room marked 'Star Artist' – and there were Matthew Trannion and Jack Spettlebury, with Hunter between them, standing in undervest and underpants, pale blue socks and brown shoes.

'I demand to know—' he began – and then he recognised Roger.

He did not speak, simply backed away a foot, his mouth dropping open. Spettlebury stood behind Roger, helping him off with his jacket, O'Malley was at a table with the contents from Hunter's pockets – the most significant being a small .22 automatic with a pearl handle. 'Fits in a special pocket in the trousers,' O'Malley said. Roger nodded, and stepped into Hunter's trousers; they were a little tight at the waist but he could get them on without difficulty.

'Better have his socks,' Roger said. 'Sorry.'

He sat down and the trousers stood the strain of bending without much trouble. The change was carried out with quick efficiency, O'Malley handing him each item, briskly explaining where it should go.

'Keys: left hand trousers. . . wallet, inside breast. . . hundred pounds folded, left hip. . .loose change, right hand trouser. . . watch, left wrist. . . penknife, right hip, examine it when you've got a chance, it looks as if it's more than a knife. . . credit cards, ticket pocket inside jacket. . . There's a single key he won't explain, in the wallet. . . driving licence, the lot.'

Roger pulled on the other man's socks, tried the shoes, then decided to wear his own. He put the automatic in the inside waistband pocket: it fitted so snugly Roger was hardly aware of it.

'You crazy fool, you'll never get away with it,' Hunter said in a high-pitched voice.

'Now you're getting too excited,' Matthew Trannion said, and before Hunter realised what was happening Spettlebury pushed his sleeve back and Trannion gave him a shot from a disposable hypodermic syringe. Hunter stared down at the tiny wound as if in dread. 'Just put you to sleep for an hour or two,' Trannion said.

'*Are we ready?*' breathed Spettlebury.

'I'm ready,' Roger said.

'This way.' Spettlebury led him outside, but they had gone only a few steps when a man in white tie and tails came forward: it was Peter Calk, looking every inch a waiter. 'I'll take you to your table,' he said. 'The Defoe woman is there - Clara *Dee*, remember. From then on, you're on your own.'

*   *   *

He was not Roger West: he was Rake Hunter.

A long way back in his police career something similar to this had happened to him but not really like this; and not suddenly being plunged into the glare of floodlights. For that was what it seemed. A troupe of dancers, all tiny, all topless, had just finished their routine performance, and were running towards the wings – towards Roger, For a few awful seconds the glare of those spotlights were on him; red, yellow, blue, pink, green. There was a roar of applause. The girls, all wearing their set grins, brushed past him. Calk said in a clear voice:

'I am sorry, Mr. Hunter.'

Hunter, remember Hunter, Hunter!

Calk threaded his way among the tables. Roger was conscious of many glances coming his way. Hunter, Hunter. A whisper came, clear: '*There's Rake Hunter.*' A waiter dodged back into his path then out of the way. 'I'm sorry, Mr Hunter.' They reached the dance floor, where a young man with glossy black hair was saying into the microphone: 'We invite you all to dance to the Moon Desert Serenaders.' No one moved. Across the floor was a redheaded girl. Good lord! thought Roger, she couldn't be more than seventeen or eighteen. *Rake* Hunter. She was smiling at him with her head on one side and there was a hint of reproach in her manner. Calk pulled back a chair.

'I am sorry you were delayed, Mr Hunter.'

'Forget it,' Roger said. Instead of sitting down he moved behind the girl and rubbed his thumb gently on the nape of her neck, and then kissed her there, lightly. At last, he sat down.

'I forgive you,' she said.

'You're telling me, Clara Dee,' Roger replied, and she gave a little grimace. Almost at once a waiter brought him a minute steak and a lobster salad for Clara. She ate delicately; she wasn't a beauty but she was full-bosomed and she had come-hither eyes. He was glad to be able to sit. Relief that he had passed this first trial surged over him. The girl obviously had no doubts about his identity. Nor had any of the waiters. Dancers on the tiny floor looked down at them, some whispering, their lips scarcely moving; people at nearby tables stared. This was really being a celebrity.

The steak and the french fried potatoes melted in his mouth, but he hardly tasted them. He drank one glass of champagne, filling his glass from time to time. Clara did little more than sip. The Moon Desert Serenaders slipped into a tango, and Clara leaned towards him.

'Shall we dance, Rakey?'

He hadn't danced a tango for years.

'Why don't we wait until we get that one about the swans, baby?'

She laughed. She had fine colouring and good teeth, and the tip of her tongue glistened.

'They won't play a waltz here, Rakey, you know that.'

He hesitated again; and then he took the plunge. 'C'mon, then,' he said, and stood up as the girl jumped to her feet. *Tango, tango, how did you do the tango*? They reached the floor as he began to get attuned to the sound and beat of the music. A police ball, not Janet, another policeman's wife. *Let him remember the steps.* Suddenly he found himself dancing. The pressure of her bosom was like the softness of down, the lightness of her movements almost unbelievable; it was like dancing with a cloud. She was smiling up into his face with obvious pleasure, and whispered: *'You've been taking lessons, baby.'* He laughed and retorted: 'It must be the champagne.' 'I always told you you were a natural dancer, if only you'd let yourself go,' she said.

He was actually sorry when the music stopped and they went back to their table. He had obviously gone down well with Clara. He allowed himself to relax enough to eat and begin to enjoy, a concoction of fresh strawberries and thick, whipped cream when a man whose photograph he had seen and memorised a hundred times came up to the table. The awful thing was that he knew this man was at the Lowndes Square house and held some special position but he could not remember his name.

'You're needed back at the house, boss,' the man said. 'There's trouble.'

17

Recall

TROUBLE.

It could be one of a hundred things, it could even be this man's way of saying that he knew the real Hunter had been arrested, that he was talking to a phoney. *Trouble*. What was his name? He was a small man with sharp but not unhandsome features and long, curling eyelashes. No one else was near.

'Oh, Curly, not now,' Clara protested. 'We were just beginning to enjoy ourselves.'

Curly! Curly, because of his sweeping eyelashes: Curly or Dai Lloyd. He shot Clara a look of utter contempt, then looked back and repeated to Roger: 'There's trouble, boss. Big trouble.'

'I'll come,' Roger said.

'But the evening's only just started!'

'Why don't you stay and give yourself a good time?' demanded Curly Lloyd.

Curly was a trouble-shooter; not the only one, but perhaps the most important of the men who served the group. He was quick with a gun, good with a knife. It was said he had the quality of evil in him, that he was a man who enjoyed causing pain for the sake of it.

Roger said: 'Don't take it out on Clara Dee, Curly,' and put a hand to help the girl to her feet. Another manager whom Roger hadn't seen before came forward, was sorry they had to go so early, hoped it was not the fault of the Club.

'The Club's all right,' Roger said.

'Boss,' said Curly, 'you ought to send the chick home in a cab, or any place she can't hear what I have to tell you.'

'Curly,' Roger said, his voice rising. 'Since when have you been doing the thinking for me?'

'I'm not thinking, boss, I'm just advising you.'

Thing to remember, thought Roger: he is not afraid of Hunter. Why? Since he himself had made an issue of it, he had to stand by his point or give way. Suddenly he was sure that Hunter would not have given way.

He said: 'I'll take Clara home. You be there as soon as I am.' He nodded to the waiting driver of his car, helped Clara in, and was not surprised when she put her face up to be kissed. He kissed her lightly, and said: 'You're going to be lonely tonight, honey. The moment you get back you'll go up to my room and then to yours. Understood?'

'You're not going to let *him* push you around, are you?'

'No,' Roger said.

'Rakey,' said Clara, 'you know it's coming to a showdown, don't you?'

His heart began to hammer.

'Who are you to talk to me about showdowns?'

'Remember me,' she said, and giggled. 'Little Clara Dee, everything happens to me. You watch out for Curly.'

'I watch out for myself,' Roger said.

'That's the way I like to hear you talk,' Clara said.

'Watch out for Number One. Rakey, did you ever think Curly was a man with ambitions?'

'What ambitions?'

'He may not be the world's great lover boy but he'd sure like to try.'

'Clara, you're crazy,' Roger said. 'Curly wouldn't try to push me aside – he wouldn't have the guts for one thing or the knowhow for another.'

'Rakey,' Clara Defoe said, and kissed his cheek. 'You're a big, big, *big* man but you don't know a thing about the men who work for you. No, sir, not a thing. Let me tell you something: never turn your back on Curly if you're alone in a room together.'

'I wouldn't turn my back on Curly if there was a crowd in the room,' Roger said.

She giggled again; he was surprised that so little drink appeared to have gone to her head. He wanted her sober, at least sober enough to take him up to his room so that he could at least see the physical aspects of the house he knew only from its plans. As they turned into Lowndes Square he gripped her hands tightly, and she woke.

'We're here,' he said.

He had never known his heart to beat as it beat now; not exactly hammering, but getting along that way. The car pulled up, and a taxi turned the corner behind them. *Curly?* The chauffeur opened the door and helped first Roger and then the girl out. He put his hand on her elbow and they went together up four steps which led to a big, black front door. This opened as they reached the porch, and a young and pretty woman said: 'Hallo, sir.'

She would be Diana, one of three 'servants' who worked at the house.

'Diana,' he grunted, and went in.

The hall was crowded with furniture, and he was instantly amazed, because some of the pieces even he, no specialist in antiques, recognised as stolen. And there was at least one stolen Utrillo at the foot of the staircase. Thanks be, no one else appeared, and they went up a wide central staircase which had passages at either side and a gallery all round. Even here the quality of the furnishing and of the paintings was as great as that possessed by any millionaire.

For 'his' room they should turn right. They did. Now his room should be first right, overlooking the square; and Clara opened the first door to the right for him with a mock curtsy; she was really a likeable little minx.

'Can't we have just *ten* minutes together?' she cooed.

'It's the half-hour it takes me to recover that I can't afford,' Roger said. 'Run along, honey. If I can come and see you later, I will.'

She went out of the room and into one immediately opposite. He strode to the door in a corner of his room; it opened onto a sumptuous bathroom, of greens and pale greys and silver. No other door led from it, and the window was shuttered, all the light coming from concealed fluorescent lighting. He turned back to the bedroom, and as he did so the telephone bell rang.

It was by the side of a huge bed, caparisoned in gold and purple, with a buttoned headboard. There were several extensions, at the sides of easy chairs and one by a built-in wardrobe which stretched from wall to wall.

He lifted the receiver and growled: 'What is it?'

'When are you going to stop fooling around with that woman and come down here?' a man's voice demanded.

'I'm not fooling with Clara Dee, I'm just getting madder and madder with Curly,' Roger said, and prayed that he had the cadence of Hunter's voice right.

'What's Curly done?'

'Send him up to me and—'

'Have you gone crazy? There's big trouble, and—'

'Sessil,' said Roger with great care, 'the biggest trouble that can happen to us is letting a piker like Curly get away with anything. That way we wouldn't know who was boss and we wouldn't know who we could trust.' He would say 'who', wouldn't he - not 'whom'?

'We can trust Curly, for heaven's sake!'

'*I* can't trust Curly,' Roger said. 'Send him up.'

As he put the receiver down, not heavily but sharply enough for no one to doubt that he meant exactly what he said, he realised his 'Sessil' had been right; had the caller been someone else he would not have let the slip pass. Whether he was right to ride Curly he couldn't yet be sure; what was certain was that from the moment of his appearance at the Moon Desert Club he had acted as if he were the boss, no matter how often he used the word 'boss' to Roger. If all he had learned of the man's character was right, this was the way to play his hand.

There was another reason for wanting Curly here: he, Roger, needed someone to guide him to where the others were.

He found a box of an expensive Turkish brand of cigarettes and filled his gold cigarette case with them. The case fitted tightly in his pocket; everything was a little too snug. He lit a cigarette, and gave a few puffs, then immediately stubbed it out on an ashtray made like the valley between a woman's breasts.

There was a tap at the door.

'C'm on in,' he called, and the door opened, and Curly appeared.

He had no doubt at all that there was a change in the man's manner. Before, there had been something aggressive and insolent in his expression; now, he was impassive. He had dark grey – slate-grey – eyes. It was impossible to be sure, but Roger thought there was a hint of apprehension in them. But it was quickly obvious that there was no subservience in Curly's manner.

'You want me?' he demanded.

'I want you,' Roger said, 'and I want you once and for all to know you can't fool this baby. Next time you bring a message to me when I'm out dining, you send message and ask if it's okay. Get me?'

'I get you.'

'And next time I'm with a chick, leave insulting her to me. I've been letting you get away with too much, Curly, because you've been with me a long time and, waal, let's face it, I've got used to having you around. But I don't want you doing things for me – I'll tell you what I want done. Get me on *that*, Curly?'

'I get you good,' Curly said.

'Keep it that way, and we've a lot of long years to work together,' said Roger. He paused for a moment, and then went on: 'C'm on. Let's go down.'

Curly gave him a prolonged stare, and then went out, leading the way down the main stairs, round to the right, then to what looked like a blank wall underneath the stairs. He pressed a button and a door slid open, showing a lift cell. For a wild moment Roger wondered if this were a trick, but he went inside and Curly followed, pressing the bottom one of three buttons. The lift moved slowly, and when it came to a standstill the doors opened automatically.

Roger had no immediate cause for alarm.

The lift opened onto a richly furnished room, with a dark gold carpet, some fine old furniture, not least the refectory table standing in front of a huge fireplace with a carved wood surround. The carving, even from this distance, looked like that of master craftsmen.

The reredos of a church had been brought in here.

Pictures, all old masters, a van Dyck, a Gainsborough – my God, thought Roger, a Titian; no one in history had ever been able to catch that particular dark golden hue. *He must not show surprise.* Over by a Jacobean chiffonier were several chairs covered with blue velvet; on the chiffonier were bottles, by the side of the chairs small tables.

Cecil Smith sat at one; a tall man with waxed moustaches and a small waxed beard, a pale face, sparse hair coiffured, wearing a suit of early Edwardian cut. He was the extreme of elegance. Opposite him Pilaski sat like a piece of solid rock carved by a sculptor who slammed his hammer on his chisel and had not cared too much which pieces were hewn. His face was very slightly lopsided. His breathing held the ghost of a whistle.

Beyond these two men was a third, identical chair, obviously his, and a question rose distractingly in his mind. Which way would Hunter enter the room? Round the back of one or the other, or in between the two men? He felt perspiration break out on his forehead as he walked straight to, and then between, them and sat down on the chair. By his side was a bottle of whisky, a finely-cut crystal jug of water and a glass. The others had ice, but he none.

'What has Curly done to offend you?' demanded Smith.

'We haff no time to talk of that now,' Pilaski said; he had a very hard, grating voice, as if his larynx was made of rock, also. 'Rake, we haff big trouble.'

'What trouble?'

'There is talk of *your* arrest.'

'You're crazy!' Roger exclaimed.

'I tell you the truth and you say it is crazy. *I* say it is true. There is talk of a decision by Scotland Yard to arrest you.'

'How do you know it's not just rumour?' demanded Roger.

'Our information comes from Scotland Yard, of course,' Pilaski declared. 'A man – the Commissioner – was heard to say you should be arrested on some charge and you should be questioned. It is not crazy, it is fact.'

On the tip of Roger's tongue was the question: Who at Scotland Yard told you this? He bit the question back, for obviously he should know the informant; one of his tasks here must be to find out who the informant was. Now he could only sit and watch these men and wonder what was in their minds.

Smith said: 'There is only one thing to do.'

'Dat is so,' agreed Pilaski. 'You must go from this house and from London at once. There must be no chance that they arrest you. Nor is there time to waste – you have to go tonight. *Now.*'

18

No Time Like The Present

THE POLE GLARED at Roger, as if in accusation; the exquisitely dressed Englishman looked at him appealingly, as if he were saying: You know this is the only possible thing to do. Roger looked away from them and poured himself a weak whisky, then sipped before he looked from one to the other.

'I'll admit one thing,' he said. 'You're not crazy, Akka.'

'So! You will go?'

'Perhaps. But I'm not going to be frightened out of England by one rumour. Did Curly give you this report?'

'Yes,' Smith answered. 'Yes, he did.'

'Have you talked to the man who told him?'

'He was telephoned. There is no one else to talk to.'

Roger appeared to be – and indeed, was – deeply meditating, then he shook his head.

'I'm slipping,' he said.

'What does zat mean?' demanded Pilaski.

'It means I shouldn't allow Curly to get into a position where he can make you two believe he's the only one who can contact Scotland Yard.'

'Well, who else can?' demanded Smith.

'*I* can,' Roger said. 'Akka, I told you, Curly is very

163

ambitious. And I told you that, Cecil. Too ambitious. If I'm not here, who joins the two of you? If I am driven out who can make contact with our distributors and buyers overseas? If I'm not here, who will our visitors talk to – which of our agents overseas can talk to someone who *knows* the situation? Do you know it, Akka?'

Slowly, frowning, doubtful, Pilaski said: 'No, I do not.'

'Cecil?'

'That's your job, and you know it.'

'Not Curly's.'

'Rake,' Smith said, 'I want to know exactly what you mean.'

'Also, I want to know,' said Pilaski.

'I'll tell you exactly what I mean,' Roger said. He picked up his glass and drank with a show of ease. 'If I were to be sent out of England you two would be in Curly's hands. He's the only one barring myself who could organise things. He would thus be in sole command. *So,* I am not going out of this place until I have a lot more evidence than there is yet.'

'But what can we do?' demanded Pilaski.

Roger said: 'We can check on Curly. Put him to the test.'

'But *how?*' demanded Cecil Smith.

'Have him bring his police pal here,' Roger said.

'But what good would that do?' demanded Smith.

'We could talk to this man and we could make up our own minds whether he's telling the truth,' Roger said. 'He can stand here in this room and answer our questions. Is that good enough?'

'If—' began Pilaski.

'There's no "if" about it,' Roger said roughly. 'If Curly can't get his man here, then Curly doesn't have a contact.'

'But in the past—'

'What has he done so wonderful in the past?' demanded Roger, but now his heart was thumping again, for this was deadly ground. He should know the answer. It could be taken as a rhetorical question but Pilaski was the most literal-minded of men. He was staring, frowning. If Cecil Smith didn't speak, then the door of suspicion would soon begin to open – and once doubts began to creep in they would soon become a flood.

'If it weren't for Curly's contact at the Yard, we couldn't have pulled off the coups we have,' Smith protested. 'He's told us the weakest men most likely to take a cut, and he's pointed a finger at a dozen we've been able to kidnap and impersonate. They were real, Rake.'

West stared at him, aware of the stare that was almost a glower from Pilaski, and then said: 'Yes, but how real was West?'

'That's different.'

'He said he could fix it for me to take West's place for a while and then he changed his mind.'

'Something went wrong,' protested Cecil Smith.

'*Curly's* gone wrong,' retorted Roger. 'And I know how he's gone wrong. He wants my job. It's as simple as that. And he got cold feet over West and had him killed – my *God*. What do you fellas have for minds? He got us to kill West, and if that wasn't *asking* for trouble for me, what was? I tell you Curly is playing a game that stinks. Make him send for his informant at Scotland Yard.'

There was a long, tense silence; and then Pilaski pressed a bell push, and a few moments later, Curly came in.

*   *   *

He stood at the far end of the room, listening. He did not look as if he had been drinking, or that he had changed his attitude; except that there now seemed no doubt of the fear in his eyes. The men he faced did not tell him of their suspicions, simply that Hunter was not satisfied with the reliability of the report.

'So, we want to talk to your informant ourselves,' Smith said.

For the first time, Curly's expression showed real alarm; his hands clenched and his arms rose in front of his chest, as if to fend off some physical attack.

'But I can't bring the man here!'

'What iss to stop you?' demanded Pilaski.

'He's at the Yard, he would have to make an excuse to get away.'

'Or do you make der excuse *not* to bring him away.'

'I tell you it would be madness. He has other work to do, he just can't walk out of his office at a moment's notice!'

'Curly, boy,' Roger said softly, 'I think you're lying.'

'I'm telling you God's truth!'

'I don't think any contact at Scotland Yard told you there was any talk of arresting me. I think you thought that up so as to get rid of me.'

'That's not true,' Curly said. 'You - *you're* getting soft.'

'So I'm getting soft,' Roger echoed, gently.

'You used to be damned good but now you're

careless. Different floosies every other night, big
presents – why you gave one of them a ring that had
been stolen on one of our jobs. You've got so careless
the police couldn't help but begin to get after you.'

'And you, Curly boy, decided you would give them
a helping hand,' said Roger. 'Get me out of the way
and you could take over. And you would be better than
me, of course, you would be the strong man of the
outfit. Not so fast, not so easily, Curly. Get your
informant over from the Yard, quick, or kiss the world
goodbye.'

Lloyd drew in a hissing breath.

Then he said: 'I'll try to get him, but it's madness.
I'll go and telephone outside, and—'

Roger pointed to a small chair next to a telephone,
and said playfully: 'What's the matter, Curly boy?
Don't you want an audience? You sit there and
telephone these bosom friends of yours at Scotland
Yard while we're listening. And don't waste time, we
may all be in a hurry.'

If there was a man at Scotland Yard—

If there was a man there who sold information to
Curly—

Then Curly would soon have to ask for him by
name.

* * *

Curly was breathing very hard, the drawing in, and
expulsion, of breath being clearly heard.

Roger had a dozen causes for fear, and one for hope.
The other two men, concentrating on Curly, were
ignoring him. But if the accusations redoubled on his
own head, what would happen?

But there was another point of view.

Nearly every piece of furniture in this underground room was priceless; and he recognised a dozen pieces, stolen from great houses and from museums. All he had to do was bring the police here now.

No: not just that.

He had to find the records; had to find how they operated. He had expected it to take weeks, even months, each day in deadly danger, but now—

'I have to call through the Yard Exchange,' Curly said in a thin voice. 'If I ask the wrong question, if the other man gets nervous—'

'What would make him nervous?' demanded Roger.

'I never call him at the Yard. Never. He - he might not even believe it was me calling.'

'Curly,' Roger said. 'You'd better try. Because I don't believe there's any call out for my arrest. I believe you're lying in your teeth, Curly. I want to know what you've been up to.'

'Nothing, I tell you, nothing. You've been whoring around, someone had to keep an eye on things.'

Roger said: 'What things?' And when Curly didn't answer he demanded: 'Why did you fix those attacks on West? Why did you kill him? There's something you haven't told us, and—'

'*You ordered the attacks on West!*' screamed Curly. '*You told me to do it. What are you trying to do?*'

Roger sprang at him – and as he sprang remembered that in anger Hunter's voice squeaked. It wasn't easy and it sounded phoney in his own ears; there was no way of being sure how it sounded in theirs.

'That's finished you, you punk!' he screeched. 'My God how far will you go to try to take over from me?

And what else have you been taking over? Come on, let's see.' He gripped Curly by the right wrist with a hold from which the other could not free himself, and screamed at Smith and Pilaski: 'It's time we checked what's going on, it's time we searched the hiding places – my God, he could have fixed the records, he could have been cashing in!'

He relaxed his hold for a fraction.

Curly pulled himself free and snatched a gun from his pocket, the inevitable weapon, the inevitable crisis. Aware of it, having prompted it, Roger swung the whisky bottle at the man's forearm, bullet and bottle met, the bottle smashed, and before Curly could stagger from the force of the blow, Roger hit him beneath the chin.

It was the blow with which Martin had floored Coppell.

It sent this man rocking back on his heels, and then toppling to the floor, the gun falling by his side. For a few moments there was no other sound but the breathing of the three men. Then Pilaski went down on one knee, felt for Curly's pulse and nodded.

'First, we put him where he can do no harm,' he said. 'Den, we go and check all der places. There is something badly wrong, that is clear.'

They half-carried, half-dragged, the unconscious man towards a door in a corner; it led to a cloakroom with a ventilation shaft but no windows. Pilaski turned the lock on this and put this key away with great satisfaction.

'Now,' he said, 'everywhere we go. Smit' you agree?'

'I couldn't agree more,' said Cecil Smith.

Both men were looking at Roger; both were obviously expecting him to lead the way. He curled the left side of his mouth in the way for which Hunter was famous. He said:

'Okay, what are we waiting for?'

'You lead us,' said Pilaski.

'I lead you *tonight* – after what you heard that guy say? What do you think I am?' demanded Roger. 'Tired of living? You two lead the way. You two do the checking.' He put his hand into his right-hand trouser pocket and drew out his keys. He dangled them in front of Pilaski, without speaking, and slowly Pilaski took them.

And he led the way to the lift in the corner. They couldn't go down – if the lift buttons were a true indication – so they had to go up. Cecil Smith pressed the button marked *One*: the floor beneath the ground floor. They stepped out of the lift and Smith turned right. Pilaski opened one door with a key from those on Roger's ring, and switched on a light. It was a small office, with fireproof filing cabinets about three walls, a central door in the fourth wall. Pilaski went to the desk, selected another of the keys and as he twisted, asked:

'Before, only you and Curly have opened this drawer.'

'Now you have,' Roger said.

The drawer opened. Pilaski hesitated and then pressed one side and a secret compartment opened. From this he took a much larger ring of keys. He held these in front of him and said: 'We go.'

'We ought to start here,' Roger said. 'We ought to check that the records are straight. There was a job in Pimlico last night, a van load of cigarettes was taken. Is it entered?'

Pilaski said: 'You open the drawer, den, for the files.'
You open the drawer.

There were dozens in here and no way of being absolutely certain that any one contained the records of last night's thefts. And knowing the records he must be able to go straight to the right drawer.

He could take a chance.

There was a sticker on each drawer but too far away for him to read. He pursed his lips and then moved towards the nearest filing cabinet. He heard Pilaski draw in a sharp, hissing breath. He saw Cecil Smith drop his hand to his pocket and take out a flick knife. He knew that they had realised at last that he was not the real Hunter. This move had given him away, but they were ready for him, and if he showed any fight now he would not have a chance. So he continued on his way to the drawer. The automatic pistol was snug against his waist, and it would take him seconds to get it out. The truth was that from this moment on he did not really stand a chance.

He stopped, a foot from the filing cabinet, and said as if to himself: 'I told him to move it.' He ignored the others and the knife was now hidden in Smith's hand. He saw that Pilaski's hand was in his pocket, undoubtedly about the handle of a gun. He moved from cabinet to cabinet, and as he began to speak his voice started to squeak:

'The double-crossing rat! I told him I wanted all of these moved, too many people knew where each cabinet was. I tell you that man is trying to take over.'

'I'll tell you something,' Pilaski said. 'I do not believe you.' He drew his hand from his pocket, and in it was a gun, larger than the one in Roger's waistband, heavy, short-barrelled, pointed uncompromisingly at Roger's chest. 'You do not know this place. Always you find some excuse for another to find what you want.'

'That's right,' Cecil Smith said, in a tense voice. He pressed his knife and the blade shot out. 'Who are you?'

There *was* no chance. Short of a miracle, they would kill him, whether he told them who he was or not. If he told them he was West they would have to get out of here quickly - but they could not let him live.

Then he saw the door, behind them, opening so slowly that it could only be furtively; by someone who did not want them to know he was there.

19

The Long Arm of the Police

ROGER SAW THE door opening but did not let himself dwell on it; saw the gun but knew that it was there, for the moment, as a threat: as a way of making him talk; and Smith's knife was there, too, for just that purpose.

He said: 'So I can't fool you.'

'No, you cannot fool us any longer,' said Pilaski. 'Who are you?'

'I can throw this knife,' declared Cecil Smith. 'I can bury it in just about any part of your body. Who are you? And where is Hunter?'

The door was opening wider; a hand appeared, and in the hand a gun. Who so slowly if it was not someone who had come to help him?

He said very clearly: 'Rake Hunter is where he should have been for a long time. Under arrest. I am—'

'You are *West*!' cried Pilaski.

There was the moment in which to act, the moment when they were both so thunderstruck that momentarily they could not move. And he went forward like a bullet at Smith, who was nearer, who drew his knife arm back mechanically but did not throw. Roger crashed into him, reaching up for the hand which held the knife, twisting until Smith screeched and it fell. Resisting the impulse to pick it up, he hugged the man

173

tightly to him as a shield between himself and Pilaski.

Pilaski fired: once.

Smith gave a little cough of sound as his body moved convulsively in Roger's arms.

Then the door opened wider and Clara Defoe stepped in and fired at Pilaski before he realised she was there. The bullet caught his gun arm, but he turned towards her, the firearm still in his hand. Roger thrust Smith away from him and moving as fast as he would ever move, knocked Pilaski's gun to the floor.

But the man wasn't finished.

There was something in his eyes which warned Roger of that, the way he looked not towards the door but above it. He brought his knee up into Roger's groin, agonisingly, and as Roger backed helplessly away he moved towards the door. Above the light switch was some kind of push-button, above the door a grille. An alarm system, that was what he was trying to do – raise the alarm. But there was such agony in the whole of Roger's body that he could not speak, could not warn Clara, who still had the gun raised but looked ashen-faced; and unsteady.

But she fired at Pilaski's hand – once – twice.

The first bullet missed. The second struck him square in the back of the hand. He gave a cry of pain and let his hand fall to his side. Roger, bent double, still in agony, muttered:

'Make him – sit down.'

Clara, pretty Clara with her seductive figure and lovely eyes, said: 'Sit down?'

'By – by the desk.'

She motioned with the gun to Pilaski, indicating a chair. Sweat was pouring from his forehead, down his cheeks, into his eyes. He moved very slowly and there was something in his manner which alarmed Roger. 'Watch him!' Pilaski shot him a glance of sheer venom, but Roger, now able to move, pushed him into the chair and dipped his hand into the other's pocket; it closed over a gun.

Everything he, Roger did seemed to be in slow motion. The pain was less acute, but spreading everywhere through his body. He pushed Pilaski's chair close to the desk, making it difficult for him to get up. There was blood all over the back of his hand and over his fingers, soaking his coat. Yet there wasn't time to help Pilaski.

The girl came over.

'Can you cut the sleeve off his jacket?'

'Yes. But—'

'I'll apply a tourniquet,' she said. 'That way he won't bleed to death. Are you all right?'

'Recovering.' He drew a deep breath. 'Talk later. Bless you.'

She smiled back at him, a little enigmatically.

Roger picked up Cecil Smith's knife. The bullet meant for Roger had caught Smith low between the shoulders, and was probably lodged in his heart. Roger took the knife and then cut out first the sleeve of Pilaski's jacket, then the shirt. Clara was pressing above an artery high in the arm. 'Better let me have his other shirt sleeve,' she said. With this she made an impromptu tourniquet, inserting a thick ruler from the desk. All this time Pilaski was conscious, but the pain of his wound, or an accumulation of weakness, suddenly made him faint. Clara Defoe moved back from him a pace or two. She was smeared with blood; hands, arms, even her face.

She began to shiver.

'Oh, God,' she said. 'Hold me.'

She was trembling from head to foot, her teeth were chattering, and her body was cold. She didn't speak. In his firm grasp the top of her head hardly came up to his chin. Slowly she quietened down enough for him to move to the desk. Here he found a bottle of brandy, a half-filled decanter of whisky, and glasses.

He poured out a stiff drink for them both. The world seemed to be standing still. He knew with one half of his mind that they must get moving, that there was a long, long way to go, but with the other part of his mind he knew they had to have some rest, that for ten minutes at least the girl would be incapable of action.

She said: 'I – I didn't think I could go through with it – not when it came to the crunch.'

'You were magnificent.'

She laughed shakily. 'Praise from a superior officer is praise indeed.'

He looked at her in utter astonishment.

'Police Officer Defoe?'

'Deroy, actually. And Dee will do —'

'But you don't look—'

'Spare me that. I am twenty-four, Superintendent, and know exactly what I am doing. Sometimes. Shall I tell you something funny?'

'There never was a time when I needed to hear a good joke more.'

She laughed. 'You may not be able to tell it to your wife and family and I may keep it a deep dark secret myself, but – I wasn't really frightened of Rake Hunter. Or of the job. They all gave me solemn warnings and tried to scare me off before I took it on, but I thought I could handle this part all right. There was risk, but there always is, a drunk I once arrested in

Wardour Street nearly broke my neck, but none of this scared me – until tonight, that is.'

'Well, Clara Dee, what did scare you?' Roger demanded.

'Sleeping with you.' she said. 'I hope that's not too much of a blow to masculine vanity.'

'Look what I've missed,' said Roger, gallantly.

'What *we've* missed.' She laughed again. 'Tell you something else.'

'Just one thing: we have to get out of here.'

'Yes,' she said, soberly. 'Yes. Well, do you know something? You would never have played the part of Rake Hunter for long. Oh, you look alike, there's something similar even in your eyes, but – well, you're different.'

'Different?'

'What a man *is*, is as important as what he looks like. And, in time, it shows. You may have got into Hunter's clothes, but you couldn't get into his skin. Everyone would have seen that before long.' She spun round towards an inner door. 'I think this is a cloakroom.'

Running water soon proved that she was right.

Now, for a few moments, Roger was alone.

It was surprising what a long time it had been since he had been alone; really on his own as he was now. A long time since he had to make swift decisions. He had needed the rest and the brandy. Though he still felt the effects of the kick, he found he could move with complete freedom. Everything depended on the situation upstairs.

And – on whether Curly had been found.

Somehow it did not seem likely that a man like Curly could be shut up in a cloakroom and left there

without making an escape: without presenting a threat
which could lead to disaster.

What were his, Roger's, assets?

The keys to this office – and no doubt the keys to the
strong rooms and safes on this floor.

Two – no, three – guns, and perhaps a dozen bullets.
Clara.

Clara, Detective Officer Deroy.

She came out of the cloakroom, looking as near to his
original sight of her as was possible.

Really, women were incomprehensible. He would
never understand them if he lived to be a hundred.

He noted that his look of astonishment and pleasure
had been accepted as a compliment, before saying:
'And now we have to make up our minds how to get
out of here.'

'I've been thinking about that, too,' Clara said,
soberly. 'And it isn't going to be easy, because the
doors down here and below have electronic control
and *I* don't know the magic trick to unlock them.' And
then, as an afterthought, she added: 'Of course, if
Curly gets free, he can unlock them.'

She smiled but her lips were trembling, and Roger
felt the icy touch of fear.

*   *   *

He gave a little shiver, and said: 'Good for Curly.'
He felt tempted to draw the brandy bottle towards
him, but he resisted it. He thought, we are caught in
between the ground floor and a lower basement. There
are no windows, and there's only the one way into this
room. He took out the cigarettes he had filched from
Hunter's room and proffered them, and she said:

'Rakey could never understand why I preferred to smoke my own.' She took a packet of Senior Service from her handbag and he took one. They lit up.

'Thanks,' he said. 'Another man knows the way out.'

She didn't look round but said: 'Akka Pilaski?'

'Yes.'

'He would never tell us.'

'Clara,' Roger said, 'I may have to make him.'

'By some form of torture?' She shook her head slowly but quite positively. 'I don't think he has the blood and nerves of ordinary people.'

'We've seen that he has.'

Her eyes were sharp and clear and unwavering.

'He won't talk. I've heard him tell stories of how he and his friends were tortured during the war. Do you know why he became a plastic surgeon?'

Did it, could it, matter?

'No,' he said.

'To help to make some of the victims look human again after the war. Do you know they cut some of his flesh off – with pincers?'

He flinched.

'He said he only helped those who gave nothing away. *He* gave nothing away. Anyone who did was a coward. That's his rule and nothing can change him.'

'A bribe?' Roger said.

'His freedom?' She laughed. '*You* wouldn't promise what you couldn't guarantee, even if he would let us go,' she said. 'No. I hate to say it, but there really *isn't* a chance.'

Roger said: 'There is always a chance.'

'You know,' she said reflectively, 'there *is* a likeness betweeen you and Rake Hunter, after all. He didn't believe that he could ever lose, either. I'll give half my salary for a year to any charity you name if you get us out of here alive. And I mean —'

She stopped, with a catch in her breath.

Roger swung round from her and stared at the grille above the door. Crackling noises were coming from it. Not voices, not breathing, something much more like atmospherics on a radio.

Then suddenly, Curly's voice sounded, coming from the grille, pitched low, but unmistakably the man who had first realised there was something wrong about this 'Rake Hunter.'

'Now who would believe it,' he said, 'who would believe we've got the great Superintendent West as a guest in our establishment. I congratulate you, Handsome, I don't believe any other man would have got inside the house, let alone fool *me* part of the time. Let me tell you a little secret, Handsome. I didn't know there had been a switch until I was tipped off. I thought you were Hunter, getting worried about me. He had plenty of reason to worry, he was on his way out. But he didn't have anything like as much to worry about as you have, Handsome. You would never believe the things that are going to happen to you.'

20

Things That Happen

ROGER WAS AWARE of the girl watching him intently; was aware of every word the man said; aware even of the hint of laughter when he finished. Roger himself was moving towards the door, and the push-button which Pilaski had tried to reach; there were smears of blood from his wounded hand and little dried streaks of blood which had fallen from it. He pressed the bell push and there was a sharp click. He stood back and spoke towards the grille.

'You could have some surprises coming, too, Curly.'

He thought he heard a gasp; he did hear a chuckle.

'You're not bad, Handsome,' Curly said. 'You know the two-way system. But that won't do you any good.'

'Curly,' Roger said, 'I've got Clara Dee here.'

'You *have*?'

'I brought her along thinking she would give me a little moral support,' West said, and when Curly did not answer, he went on: 'I thought they were beginning to doubt me, and if anybody ought to be able to vouch for me, she should.'

'Like I said,' said Curly, 'I congratulate you, you're quite a guy. So why don't you spend your last hours on earth in her arms. You wouldn't say no, Clara Dee, would you?'

'I also have three guns and a dozen bullets,' Roger went on, 'with assorted knives. Cecil Smith is dead, and Pilaski is out of action with a shattered right hand and a bullet-hole in his left hand.'

'You're quite a cop,' Curly said. 'Now cut the cackle, and —'

'Let Clara come out, before the shooting starts,' West said.

'Let her *out*?'

'It's not her fault she got tangled up in this. She tried to help Pilaski. Let her out.'

'And leave the door open for you to follow her, I suppose.'

'You can cover the door with a dozen guns,' Roger said. 'It's her I'm worried about.'

There was a pause before Curly said: 'I'll make a deal.'

'Name it,'

'If we let her out you give yourself up,' Curly said.

'You know I can't do that. After what you've told me will happen to me.'

'Listen, West,' said Curly in a different, almost pleading voice, 'you've got a mind. Yes, sir, you've got a good mind and you've got a lot of guts. Let's talk business. With Smith gone and Hunter away for a while we need someone else, and a man inside the Yard, a highly-placed officer like you – boy, you could be just what we need! We've had all the killing we want. If we let Clara out and let her go free, will you talk?'

Roger hesitated, cupped his hands and whispered to Clara: 'Plead with me. Beg him to let you go.'

'Can you hear me?' Curly's voice was harsher.

'Loud and clear, but —'

'Let me go!' Clara cried, and the sob in her voice almost convinced West that she was speaking with desperation. 'For God's sake let me go – I wouldn't have come near the place if I'd known.' Her voice changed, she began to sob, and she actually clung to West. 'Mr West, please, I can't stand it any more. Let me go, let me —'

Her voice faded away into sobs.

'What's that I was saying about you?' called Curly. 'Quite the ladies' man, eh?'

Heavily, as if he hated making the concession, Roger said: 'All right, Curly, let her go. Out of the house, mind you, not just out of the room. I want her to telephone me when she's in the street – when I've got her message, I'll come out without a fight.'

'Why sure, sure!' Curly's voice was warm with assurance.

'Only to talk!' Roger barked. 'I'm not promising anything.'

'Why sure, Handsome, just to talk,' Curly soothed. 'But it can be a big deal – it can mean a hundred thousand pounds a year for you, free of tax. We'll let her go, and we'll talk.'

'Oh, thank God, thank God!' gasped Clara.

Roger cupped his hands about her ear. 'They'll follow and shoot you down as soon as you've telephoned. Get to a phone in a main street, dial 999 and just say: 'Handsome West says urgent an immediate raid on 413 Lowndes Square.' Then hang up as if you'd had a wrong number, and call here.'

She whispered: 'Right.'

'West,' called Curly, 'the door can be opened. You keep away from it or you'll both be hurt – badly.'

Slowly, very slowly, Clara went to the door and pulled – and it opened and there was no sound. She opened it wide enough to get through. Roger, standing back, two pistols at the ready, was prepared for the door to be flung wide open and to be shot down; but – nothing happened. He could hear Clara breathing. He heard her footsteps – and he saw the door begin to close.

* * *

Curly meant what he said.

Roger sat against the wall, thinking it out. There was no sound now – Pilaski seemed to be more dead than alive. Every second dragged. He could not be sure they had let her go. He was sure that if they did, they would give her only the chance to talk to him and then kill her. Even if she got her message through to 999 there was no certainty that whoever followed her to the call box wouldn't shoot her.

Ten minutes... twelve minutes... fourteen minutes...

They might be torturing her to make her talk; might be doing to her what had been done to Maria Consuela. My *God* what a pair of women!

Sixteen minutes...

Brrr-brrr. Brrr-brrr, Brrr—

He snatched off the receiver but he could hardly find words, his mouth and his tongue were so dry. But he said:

'Is that you, Clara?'

'Yes, yes, they let me go, I'm all right. I – I hated

running out on you, I just hated it, but they would have killed me, and – and you don't know what they will do to women, they —'

'It's all right, Clara,' Roger said. Every second, police cars were converging on the house in Lowndes Square, by now there could be no doubt that everyone concerned was alerted, every available car was heading for this spot. And Clara was fighting desperately for her own life. 'It's all right,' he repeated, 'I got you into this and I'm glad I got you out of it. Now I've got to —'

'Whatever you do don't trust Curly, whatever you do don't trust him!'

And then he heard the wail of a police siren and knew that a police car was on the way to her, and he banged down the receiver and crouched behind the desk, Pilaski's gun in his hand.

For a few seconds, nothing happened.

Then the door was drawn back and two men flung themselves in, diving for the floor so as to make themselves more difficult targets. Calmly, and with deadly aim, Roger shot them; one of them was Curly.

Roger waited, fairly sure that no one else would take a chance, but not prepared to take one himself until, in less than ten minutes, he heard a man call out in a familiar voice:

'Handsome! Are you there, Handsome?'

Roger raised his voice. He saw Curly looking at him, saw the pain reflected in Curly's eyes. He spoke not in his own but in a passable imitation of Curly's voice, and he sounded full of alarm: 'Get away, Partridge – he knows we've been working together! Get away, you haven't a chance!'

There was another silence, falling like a heavy cloak.

He saw Curly's lips twisting – whether in hate or in admiration he would never really know. A gasp of sound came from the other side of the door, and then Partridge said in a thin voice:

'It's – it's nonsense!'

'It's the truth,' Roger called. 'Curly's still alive and he has confirmed it.'

'I can't believe he'd talk!' Partridge said.

Another man spoke sharply, saying: 'I shouldn't go in there, Mr Partridge. Sergeant, fetch Mr Coppell or Mr Trannion quickly, will you. Mr Partridge!' There was the sound of a struggle and then the thud as of a body falling, followed by the man who had spoken, saying; 'Oh, my God, he's killed himself.'

*   *   *

'So,' said Sir Joseph Trevillion, 'you pulled it off again.'

'I helped,' Roger said. 'I'll want to recommend those two women officers for the highest recognition we can give them.'

'Yes, yes, all in good time,' Trevillion replied. 'Through the proper channels, eh, Commander?'

'Yes, sir,' Coppell said. 'But my oath, this place is a treasure house.'

'Lots of grieving owners and a lot of insurance companies should be very glad. Yes indeed. Well, West. You ought to go home. Your wife's been told, by the way, no need to worry about that. Overjoyed. Shall we send you back in a car? Of course, best thing. Find wagon loads of newspapermen outside, of course, cope if you can but better to give them a prepared statement on your part in this. Want to make sure they really know what a hero you are!' He gave a roguish grin and gripped Roger's hand.

'Handsome,' Coppell said.

'Yes, sir?'

'Best bloody copper we've ever had at the Yard and the one with most guts. *And* I shall say so when I leave here tonight.'

Later, Roger fought his way through the crowd of newspapermen and, helped by police, reached his car. He was leaning back with his eyes closed when by devious routes they reached Bell Street. Lights were blazing at his house and twenty or more newspapermen were there, but they did not over-press for news, wanting only a little confirmation, and the chance to show their approval. Janet and the boys were already in the hall, their faces showing just how deadly the past few hours had been. Halfway down the stairs was Anne Claire, looking sweet and appealing in a pale blue dressing-gown, her hair as feathery as a child's.

'Mr West, I couldn't possibly rest until I had told you how glad I am,' she said.

To Janet's surprise, to Richard's, to Martin's, Roger simply looked at her, his face impassive. He took in the enormous eyes, the innocence, the halo of spun hair against the landing light above her.

'Couldn't you, Anne?' he asked at last, and noted the whitening of her knuckles as she gripped the banister rail. 'I don't suppose you knew just how deadly this affair was, but you listened-in as much as you could, and passed on all the information you picked up to Superintendent Partridge.'

The colour was dying from her cheeks.

'It was on Partridge's recommendation that you came here, and I thought it a good idea because Janet gets too lonely sometimes.' He took Janet's hand. 'And even, sometimes, lets out little pieces of information which you were able to pass on. These things are true, aren't they?'

Quite suddenly, she crumpled. Martin rushed to pick her up, a distraught Martin, his face a battleground of loyalty, love and shock.

*　　*　　*

Soon, police from the Division came and charged her with divulging secret information, and took her away.

Roger went, escorted by legions of newspapermen, to the Yard. Everyone greeted him warmly, he had never known such goodwill. He went into his own office and immediately saw signs that Detective Sergeant Hadley was back on duty. He was about to ring for him when the telephone bell rang, and with his normal briskness he said: 'Roger West.'

'The handsome, heroic, Roger West,' a woman's voice said, and at the sound of that particular lilt he would never forget, he felt as if the whole world were standing still.

'Maria,' he said. 'Where are you?'

'At London Airport,' she answered. 'I'm flying back on the next flight.' When he made a sound as if to protest, she went on gently: 'It's the only possible thing to do, Roger, and you know it as well as I. I thank God you're alive and I thank you that I've no feeling of bitterness left and I don't think it will come back. Thank you, darling.'

'Maria,' he said, 'if - if I could just see you off.'

She said quietly: 'No goodbyes, Roger, but if sometime you find yourself in New York - who knows?'